RUSSIAN H

KENNETH EADE

To Tim, who believes in me and supports me through thick and thin

"Victory is no longer a truth. It is only a word to describe who is left alive in the ruins."
— Lyndon B. Johnson

"Cold War? War don't have no temperature."
— Marlon James

RUSSIAN HOLIDAY

KENNETH EADE

CHAPTER ONE

Aleppo, once an idyllic jewel between Mesopotamia and the Mediterranean, was the oldest inhabited city in Syria and one of the oldest in civilization. Robert Garcia had been in many battle zones before, but this was nothing like he had ever seen. Aleppo had been decimated. Jagged slabs of concrete hanging on the exposed bones of twisted, rusting steel, the ashes of wooden shops now reduced to cinders, broken corrugated shutters of what used to be jewelry stores, and the ruins of bombed-out, formerly splendid historical mosques, their once glittering chandeliers now hanging from the dusty rubble.

It reminded him of those surreal black and white photographs of Hiroshima and Nagasaki after the atom bomb had been dropped. Once a thriving metropolis, now a graveyard inhabited only by terrorists and their mostly unwilling civilian subjects – slaves, held captive by the boundaries of their destinies.

Robert set up his shot from the seventh floor of an abandoned, blown-out building, once part of the modern city, which could hardly be distinguished from its ancient ruins, now themselves almost completely obliterated by all the bombing. A bead of sweat from the intense heat dripped into his eye and he wiped his brow dry.

He gripped his Dragunov SVD sniper rifle and simulated the shot he was about to take, beginning his breathing protocol as he observed the place where he would send General Abu Muslim al-Basara, once the pride of Sadaam Hussein's Royal Guard, now an ISIS terrorist, to Jahannam. He watched as al-Basara's colonel spread the battle plan out on the desk. This was

5

to be their moment of glory, the day they would drive out the last of the infidels and strangle the life out of what was once the largest city near the Turkish border. The day which would pave the way for their growth to metastasize into and infect the land that had been conquered by the Romans and retaken by the Muslims – only to be forsaken again and was now sitting in the clutches of the Jewish empire of the United States.

Robert concentrated on the target zone through his sight and ran his tongue across his dry lips. In front of the building, men in flak jackets holding automatic weapons were milling around, but that wasn't going to make any difference. From 500 meters it would be a turkey shoot and he would disappear before they knew where the shots had come from. In the dead wind, the bullet would cut through the air like a hot knife through a stick of butter, finding its purchase accurately with no need for compensation in trajectory. He looked through the small window and watched the colonel studying the plans. Robert's optics were so precise, he could count the hairs on the Colonel's beard. He was target number two. *Breathe and wait, breathe and wait.*

When the prime target finally came into focus, Robert unclenched every muscle, relaxing everything except for his eye and his trigger finger. He placed the cross hairs right on the forehead of the target and squeezed, every so softly, as if he were tickling the most intimate part of a woman. He immediately fired another round to the chest as he watched the first bullet make contact, popping the general's head back, his lifeless body dropping to the ground, and then took out the surprised colonel with a shot to the head and one to the chest.

Robert abandoned his equipment, vacated what was left of the room and scurried down the seven flights of destroyed stairs, sometimes leaping over patches of nothingness as he descended. He could hear the commotion and turmoil from across the street – orders being screamed out, the roar of trucks coming closer. He slipped out the exit, and briskly walked the half block to the designated pickup area, but the pickup vehicle wasn't there.

Shit!

He knew there was no such thing as a perfect plan. Every good one fell apart in the field, especially when you depended on someone else. When it came to life or death, or anything else important, the only one you could count on was yourself.

Someone's head's gonna roll for this one.

He ducked into an alley, just as a Humvee and six Toyota trucks, courtesy of the U.S. Government, and packed with jihadists holding automatic weapons, pulled up in front of the building in a cloud of dust and piled out, invading it like an intrusion of cockroaches. Halfway down the alley, Robert pulled several bags of trash off a garbage pile, revealing a motorcycle hidden underneath. He pulled the motorbike out from under the clutter by the handlebars, and then he jumped on it and kicked it to life. The roar of its engine echoed down the alley and caught the ears of his pursuers as he flew out the other side in a cloud of exhaust. Robert's Plan B packed a punch – strapped to the back of the bike was a Fagot ATGM. He was, literally, a mobile army.

Dodging piles of rubble with rebar protruding from them like writhing snakes, and burned-out trucks and cars, he headed for higher ground. He had no Commo set, nothing to call for an extraction, and nobody would be coming for him anyway. He wasn't officially there.

Why the hell do they need a covert op in a shithole like this anyway? Why not just send in the cavalry?

He took evasive moves, but could hear the rat-a-tat-tat of the AK-47s and RPKs behind him. He looked over his shoulder and took a sharp left, leaning to the ground and almost scraping his knee to it, like a motorcycle racer, but one of the nimble Toyotas followed and was still gaining on him. Robert looked for cover. If he could find something to protect himself from their fire, he could hold his ground and fight it out with the ATGM, but it was difficult to find shelter. Most of Aleppo had been laid to waste. It was if a giant earthquake had flattened half of it to the ground. As he drove, turning randomly everywhere he could, he looked for a suitable building to hole up in and make his stand. He ducked down a street that was filled with rubble, pieces of metal siding and chunks of concrete, in order to slow the trucks' pursuit.

Damn!

Robert heard the chopping blades of a Black Hawk helicopter in the distance, looked up and could see it was coming for him.

Need to hide, need a diversion. Anything!

He ducked behind a bombed-out building, parked the bike, set up the ATGM and trained it on the helicopter, which was closing in on him fast. He could see the muzzle fire from its machine guns as the bullets pelted the buildings around him. He aimed, fired, and the Black Hawk exploded in a spectacular firebomb, raining shrapnel from a cloud of smoke.

Robert had hoped that downing the helicopter had bought him more time, but the Humvee and its convoy were still approaching. They were too close to outrun. He reloaded the AT-GM and fired a direct shot, blowing up the Humvee, and sending two of the Toyotas off the road. He hopped on the bike and zipped away, confident he had bought at least a few precious seconds.

Up ahead, Robert flew through the archway of what used to be a grand bazaar and now was nothing but a huge concrete rathole, and gunned for the opening on the other side. He maneuvered through brick and stone, pipes and crushed furniture, looking to the light at the end of the huge building which would be his salvation. That light suddenly darkened when a Humvee rolled in front of the exit. Robert saw the flash of an RPG and swung to the right side down another corridor just as the grenade exploded, raining concrete particles and dust. He jammed the throttle with his wrist all the way back in a sprint for the new exit ahead. He could see it getting closer and closer.

It's clear. Almost there, almost...

Suddenly, a Toyota truck screeched to a halt, blocking Robert's way. He veered toward a crack of opportunity on the right – an opening – and slid, the back tire hit the bumper of the Toyota, propelling Robert airborne. He landed with a thud in the street. He was, for a moment, phased, and struggled to stand up so he could make a run for it. It was impossible. When he stood up, he was staring up at the barrels of a six-man firing squad.

CHAPTER TWO

Robert moved his eyes about himself like a bird, sizing up his situation. It couldn't be worse. He knew this was the Islamic State and mercy wasn't in their mindset. The penalty for being caught was death. Nobody was going to save him. If he broke to run he would be shot in the process. This was it; it was just a matter of time. But Robert also knew time meant opportunity. After all, what more do we have than time? We measure it arbitrarily, but as we spend it, until it's used up, it is called living.

As long as I'm alive, there's a chance.

He braced himself for the shots that were surely to come, but they didn't. Instead, a mad, short man, spitting obscenities in Arabic, ordered the men not to fire. Robert spoke their language perfectly, which was one of the reasons he was perfect for this assignment. With his dark skin and black hair, he could easily pass as an Arab, or just about anyone, for that matter. He was a master of disguise, able to escape pursuit by blending in with any crowd. But it wasn't going to help him this time.

Two men pulled him from the ground and frisked him aggressively. He resisted the impulse to grab both of them and use them as human shields to bargain his way out. But ISIS could not be bargained with. They would simply shoot through both of their soldiers if need be and send Robert to hell and their two compatriots to Jannah. One of the men grabbed Robert's 9mm Glock from his shoulder holster and shoved it into his pocket. If they had been alone, Robert could have easily retrieved his weapon, shot the man and his partner dead, and reholstered the Glock. Not this time. The other man pulled his KBAR knife from his belt and his Ruger .22 from his ankle holster. Now, even with his clothes on, Robert felt he was truly naked.

The first jihadi spit in his face and punched his stomach. The second kneed him in the groin and Robert doubled over silently in pain. Underneath the pain was pure, unadulterated anger, but he was mostly mad at himself for getting caught. The little guy who was apparently now in charge stood in front of him. He smelled like a rotten corpse.

Apparently, killing his bosses made this guy a bit nervous.

"Who do you work for?"

"I'm a free agent."

The little guy punched Robert in the nose. He felt the impact, could hear it crack and sensed the warm flow of blood running from it into his mouth, but stifled any reaction from the searing pain.

"Does that help refresh your memory?"

Robert spit blood and shook his head. "No, I can't say that having my nose broken does stir up any memories."

"You are a despicable heathen."

Robert smiled under the bloody drip. "I'm that and more."

"I will be happy to see your head hanging on a spike in Naeem Square."

Robert grinned. "After me, there will come another, who will kill you and put your head right next to it."

The man grimaced. "Take this piece of shit away and prepare him for his execution."

The two goons grabbed Robert, pushed him toward one of the Toyotas, shoved him into the back of it and drove off, followed by the other trucks and a Humvee. They didn't bother blindfolding him – he wouldn't live to tell the location of their headquarters. Fifteen minutes later they rolled in to a heavily guarded compound.

Robert was handcuffed, but he wasn't given a prison cell or a last request. There would be no trial. This was going to proceed quickly. They rustled him out of the car, threw him down on his knees and set up a video camera on a tripod. Four of the armed men donned black masks and surrounded him, pointing their weapons at his head. Another stood in front of the camera. Then, the little man stepped forward.

"I should let you go free so you can thank your president for me for all this wonderful military equipment." He waved his arm around the yard, showing off the hardware. "M16s, Humvees, machine guns, M62 grenades, anti-tank missiles, howitzers, armored vehicles and personnel carriers. We couldn't fight this war without his help."

"Fuck you."

Red in the face, he screamed. "Silence while I read this statement!" He, too, donned a black mask.

"Fuck your mother, too."

The little man backhanded Robert, forcing him to the ground completely.

"Get back on your knees, *kafir*! It is time to die!"

Robert lay on the ground, not moving. Two of the armed jihadis yanked him back to his knees as the little man read his statement to the camera.

"This assassin, sent by the CIA into our country, murdered a general and colonel of our army and for that the penalty is death. Death of one man and for all of you! Since the United States has no motivation to deal with the Muslims except by force, we are replying with force, the only language you understand."

The little man stepped aside and a masked executioner stood behind Robert and raised a scimitar above his neck. Before he could strike, his head exploded and the blade fell into the dust. The little man was the next to be shot, and as he dropped to the ground, Robert slid behind his body, withdrew his 9mm Glock and shot two of the terrorists as the other two dropped to the ground from sniper fire. He took cover behind one of the vehicles as more jihadis ran out from the compound, shooting wildly in all directions. As they dropped like flies sprayed with poison, Robert joined the free for all, shooting whoever was still moving and breathing.

The military equipment which was the object of the dead little man's boasts began to explode from ATGM fire. One by one, in rapid succession, the armored vehicles and Humvees exploded, followed by the building. Robert lay low to protect himself from the flying particles of dust and metal.

Finally, a blanket of quiet fell over the compound, which had been reduced to a graveyard. Two Desert Tiger armored vehicles sped in and parked in front of Robert. A burly Russian man popped his head out of the top of one of them as its door swung open.

"Get in!"

Robert hesitated.

"Come on! We are on same side. At least for now."

The big Russian smiled and Robert stepped inside the truck.

CHAPTER THREE

The big man held out a hand to Robert. He was still smiling. Robert took the hand and felt his crushing grip as the Tiger sped away.

"My name Alexei, but people call me Lyosha."

"Bob."

"Boab?"

"No, it's pronounced *Bob,* like in *stop.* You're saying *Boab,* like in *boat.*"

"*Boab*? Like in *stoap*? Well, Boab like in stoap, it looks like your CIA left you for dead."

Robert didn't answer the question. Instead, he asked one of his own. "Where are you taking me?"

"Syrian FOB about 40 clicks from here, but only if you need ride. You are welcome to wait for CIA by side of road."

"That's okay, I'll take the ride."

"We can take you across Turkish border. No passport control."

He grinned. His conservative cut blond hair and Slavic face reminded Robert of Ilya Kuryakin on the Man from U.N.C.L.E., only twice as big. Robert thought for a second.

"What are you guys doing here, anyway?"

"I could ask you same. We are training Syrian Army and providing military equipment. Looks like you guys are providing military equipment to ISIS. That was all your stuff we just blew up, right?"

"I really don't know what they're doing. I'm a free agent."

"Well, Mr. Free Agent, everybody knows we are here. But I don't suppose anyone knows or would admit you are."

Robert didn't answer.

"We are doing same job as you – getting rid of terrorists. Problem is you guys are also supporting terrorists. All they have to do is say they try to overthrow Assad government, and they get free stuff."

"That's not what I'm doing."

"We know what you do. We have been admiring your work."

The Tiger rumbled on through the windy, dusty roads, and out of the surreal, bombed-out landscape of Aleppo.

"We call it Syria's Stalingrad."

"Looks like it."

"Boab, let's get one thing straight, okay? We are here to kill terrorists; you are here to help Syrian Army kill terrorists. You don't mess with our job and we won't mess with yours."

"That's fine. My job's done here anyway. I'm officially on vacation now."

"Vacation? You mean holiday?"

Robert nodded and the big Russian smiled. "So you do need ride."

"I guess so. Have you got a burner I can use?"

Lyosha reached into his bag and pulled out a bunch of phones. He fanned them out to Robert like a hand of cards.

"What color you like?"

Robert smiled. He grabbed one of the phones, waited for a fleeting signal, and dialed.

"It's me."

"What happened?"

"Nothing happened. That's the problem. Your pickup wasn't there."

"What about the target?"

"Taken care of."

"Give me your 20, we'll get you out of there."

"No thanks, I've already got a ride."

Robert clicked off, popped out the SIM card, and snapped it in half. Then he rolled down the window and tossed the card and the phone out into the desert.

When they arrived at the FOB, Robert drew stares from members of the Syrian army as the Tiger dispersed its Russian passengers. Robert looked back at them, wondering if they thought he was a prisoner. Lyosha slapped a big hand on his back.

"You hungry, Mr. CIA?"

"I won't refuse."

"Come with me. I show you where you can clean up and then we eat."

***

Robert showered, and found a first aid kit to fix up his nose. He stuffed his nostrils with gauze and taped it over the bridge, which looked like he was wearing some kind of a macabre Halloween mask, and tended to his cuts and scrapes with antiseptic and bandages. Then, he donned a fresh set of BDUs from the closet. They were a little baggy, no doubt because his hosts were taller than he was, but the fit worked. He wandered around, asking in Arabic where the Russians were, and was directed to the officers' mess. Lyosha saw him come in and waved.

"Hey, CIA! Get yourself a plate and come on over!"

Robert stepped up to the mess, grabbed a tray and plate and the cook filled it generously. He walked back to the table and began to slide in next to Lyosha, only to be interrupted by introductions and a short hand shaking ceremony.

"Bob, this is Slava, Yuri, Sasha and that little guy over there is Pyotr."

The "little guy" was over six feet tall. Robert felt like a Lilliputian in their presence. He shook their hands with gratitude.

"Thank you all for saving my life today."

"We can't let CIA man die, can we, *ribyata*?" There was a round of negative "*niets*," as Lyosha grabbed a bottle of Titomirov vodka and poured everyone's glass full. He raised his glass and nodded to Robert, who followed suit with his.

"To our new American friend. *Tibya zdarovia!*"

Robert clinked everyone's glass, and watched as they all slammed their payloads in less than a second. Then, he realized they were all looking at him.

"Go ahead, Boab. It won't kill you. Might help nose!"

Lyosha translated and all the Russians laughed. Robert took the shot down all at once, Russian style. It was ice cold to his lips and burned warm against the back of his throat. He looked back at Lyosha, who handed him a pickle and refilled his glass.

Robert took the pickle and bit into it as Lyosha performed the next toast in Russian and then translated for Robert. "To sending those terrorist bastards straight to hell!"

The group rumbled in approval as they clicked, slammed and exhaled briskly. They feasted on plate after plate of food between drinks and pickles, until the bottle was getting lonely. The room was spinning around Robert's head, but it felt good.

All of a sudden, Yuri broke into song. Lyosha translated the lyrics.

"Song is about space travelers, dreaming of green grass of home. Sing wiz us!"

"But I don't know the lyrics."

"Boab, you been drinking vodka wiz Russians all night. Feel your way."

"*I snitsya nam ne rokot kosmadrova*
Ne eta lendenaya snievam
A snitsya nam trava, trava i doma"

Lyosha slapped Robert's shoulder, "*Davai!*"

"*Zilonaya, zilonaya trava!*"

The tune was contagious, so Robert chimed in, slurring his *la-la-las* along with the music. As the song concluded, the vodka flowed once more, until the next song, and the next.

"Our friend Boab is going on *otdykhayat*, and so are we. So we must drink to *otdykhayat!*"

As they toasted, Robert guessed that meant they were all taking some R & R. "Where are you going?"

"Everyone goes home to see family. Slava goes to St. Petersburg, Pyotr to Ekaterinburg. Yuri is from Siberia. I'm the only one going to Moscow. Why don't you come wiz me?"

Robert shook his head. "Oh, I don't know."

"Have you ever been to Russia?"

"No."

"Then you must come. I invite you. Do you have visa?" He paused, then grinned. "Of course you do. All CIA have visa to Russia!"

He raised his glass. "*Za Moskva*! To Moscow!"

Robert slammed down his drink and chomped on another pickle. Lyosha refilled everyone's shots. Robert saw what he was doing and put a hand over the top of his glass.

"Oh, no more for me."

Lyosha ignored him, swept his hand out of the way and poured his glass full.

"Don't be silly. This is last drink. He raised his glass. "To Russian holiday!"

They toasted, drank and then Lyosha's expression turned serious.

"You know, I like you, Boab. I hope I don't have to kill you someday."

Lyosha was smiling. Robert smiled back, but kept his response to himself.

"It was joke, CIA, joke!"

He translated the joke to his buddies, and they all erupted in laughter, including Robert. They all slammed their shots. But the jovial mood was underscored by reality. Robert had been thinking exactly the same thing.

CHAPTER FOUR

It was a desolate trek through ancient ruins and olive orchards to the Syrian border crossing of Bab al-Hawa, where each band of ne'er-do-wells was trying to accomplish some nefarious task. There were smoldering masses of refugees trying to escape from Syria, weapons smugglers trying to bring weapons and fighters in, and oil and gas smugglers trying to get ISIS oil and gas out. The band of Russian brothers spoke in Russian, of course. They talked about their girlfriends back home and what they planned to do on their holiday, but Lyosha translated what he thought would be the most interesting for Robert.

"So Boab, do you have someone?'

"Me, no, nobody."

"Good looking *chilavek* like you? Come on, you must have left million broken hearts back home."

"Just a dog."

"You have dog? What kind?"

"I don't know. Just an ugly old dog. Back home we call 'em Heinz 57s. He showed up on my doorstep one day and wouldn't go away."

"Your dog's name Heinz?"

"No, actually, it's Butthead."

"Butthead? Like Ass-face?"

"Well, kind of. His face looks a little like his ass, and vice-versa."

Lyosha shrugged. "Girl much better than dog. She don't pee on rug and you don't have to take her outside, unless you want of course. I introduce you to girl in Moscow. If she don't steal your heart, at least you have lot of fun."

Lyosha translated for his friends, who laughed heartily.

"We have most beautiful girls in Russia. More girls than man. It is paradise for man, believe me."

The traffic began to slow to a stop. Yuri moved off onto the right shoulder and made his own little freeway, passing long lines of trucks and buses, and following the signs for diplomatic crossings as they sped by masses of people sitting off the sides of the road in their own filth. A few tents, but mostly whole families parked on blankets among the trees. Lyosha motioned with his head toward the window.

"Those people nobody care about. They have nowhere to go. It's all about money, my friend."

Robert nodded. He knew it was all about money. He made his killing people, and couldn't understand Lyosha's concern for those who weren't strong enough to make their own place in this scum-filled world. He looked out the window at them: Young men, old men and women sitting around, and children running around, playing in the dirt.

I guess I'm lucky I wasn't born here.

Their crossing was without incident, as Lyosha had promised. A short while later, they were exchanging the Tigers for civilian transportation and heading for the idyllic Mediterranean city of Iskenderun, formerly known as Alexandria.

***

Iskanderun's palm-lined promenade was inviting, as was the cool breeze that drifted in from the sea, but Robert had only one stop he wanted to make before the airport.

"Yuri, could you please stop over there at Societe Generale?"

"You going to rob bank, Boab? Then we all split money."

"Just taking what's mine."

"Isn't that what your Dalton Brothers said when they robbed banks in Wild West?"

Robert grinned and nodded. "I suppose it was." They pulled up in front of the bank and Robert got out. He hung back and leaned into the window. "Just be a minute."

Before going into the bank, Robert broke open the lining of his jacket and fished out a small key. He entered the lobby and checked in with the safety deposit box teller. After signing in, he gave the teller his key and she opened a slot in the vault and withdrew a medium sized box, which Robert took into the private room. He scanned the corners of the room for any security cameras and found one blinking at him. He flashed his laser pointer at it, settling it at the proper angle to block the camera while he opened the box. Inside was the usual espionage go-bag contents packed in a small backpack: Passports from various European countries, stacks of cash in euros and dollars, a satellite phone, some burner phones, and his favorite – the Glock 19 with three clips. He grabbed some bricks of euros and dollars, one of the passports that he (not they) had secured, and a couple of the burners, and stuffed them into the backpack. He picked up and fondled the Glock and then put it back down.

Not this time, baby. Too dangerous to go into Russia with a gun.

He closed the box and switched off the laser.

***

An alarm went off at the state-of-the-art operations area of the National Counterterrorism Center at the same time its counterpart went off at CIA headquarters in Langley. The technician noted the information, then left the hi-tech control room with its dozens of computer terminals and large video screens and headed for the boss' office. Nathan Anderson had left explicit instructions to be informed of any new developments. His agency, NCTC, had compiled the finest database in the world on suspected terrorists. The only problem is there was nothing they could do with the data except pass it on to their other acronymic counterparts.

It was an agency designed to combat terrorism which had no enforcement power of its own and could only be described as impotent. But Anderson, its head, an Obama appointee, was looking for a dose of Viagra to inflate the agency's importance. Robert Garcia, also known in social media by his pseudonym, *Paladine*, was his pet project. Even though Robert reported to the CIA, Anderson made sure he was informed of his status on a regular basis. They had Robert by the balls; an indentured servitude of sorts, but only for a limited time. Robert could kill his way back to freedom and get paid for it as well.

The technician entered Anderson's office and handed him the status report, encrusted with the CIA's special cryptogram on Robert: PAL.

"Your status report on PAL, sir."

Anderson looked up at the technician, trying to hide his excitement. Any news on Robert always perked him up.

"Thank you."

The technician set the report on Anderson's desk and he waited until he was out to pick it up.

***

Not far away, at a similar, yet older installation, Ted Barnard, the head of the CIA, was getting the same briefing from one of his agents.

"We just got a report that PAL has entered Russia."

Barnard almost choked on his coffee. He set the cup down and licked his lips.

"Russia?"

"One of his passports – the one he thinks we don't know about – just scanned through at Sheremetyevo."

"What's he doing in Moscow?"

"I don't know, sir. I hear he was pretty peeved when his pickup didn't happen in Aleppo. Do you think maybe he went rogue?"

"No. Once he completed his assignment we'd agreed he could take some time off. He's probably just blowing off steam."

"But in Moscow?"

"Well, they say the best hookers are from Eastern Europe."

Barnard chuckled, suppressing his anger and embarrassment. An operative like Robert, even an illegal one they would never acknowledge, could be tortured and be compelled to reveal vital secret information. As long as he was there, he was more of a liability than he normally was.

"I'll let you know when we receive a new development."

"You do that. Oh, and have him paid a visit when he gets back home – remind him who he really works for."

The agent nodded and left the office, closing the door behind him. Barnard looked up at his wall at the photograph of himself with the president. He didn't trust Robert and he was worried. The hands of power at the CIA had changed too frequently during the past decade, from scandal to scandal. He wasn't about to be the next fall guy.

CHAPTER FIVE

A blank stare, green eyes flicked up and down, up and down. The Border Service guard was taking her time with Robert's passport. She had already scanned it, but kept looking down at his picture and flashing her green eyes back up at him. He stayed calm, cool and collected as she studied him with emotionless expression. If there was an alert out on him as a suspected CIA operative, he would deal with it, one step at a time. Robert's realm was the undercurrent of the illegitimate space of covert operations – the dirty little (and big) things the government does but doesn't want to admit to. One of the consequences of working in that space is getting caught and having your own country turn its back on you. Finally, she printed his immigration card, gave it to him to sign, returned his passport, and he was done.

Lyosha was standing, impatiently outside the passport control booth . "What hell took you so long?"

"Not my country, you tell me."

"Doesn't matter. Moscow waits."

Robert didn't have any bags – only the small backpack – and Lyosha's had already been picked up, so it was a quick exit to curbside and an even quicker pickup in a shiny black Mercedes 600.

"Nice ride."

Lyosha tipped his head toward the dark, sleek vehicle. "Their car. On salary they pay me, I can't afford Russian Volga." Robert slid into the backseat and Lyosha into the front. He turned to the driver and said, "*Piekhele*," and the car took off smoothly, but with what seemed like the speed of a drag racer.

"They probably know you're in Moscow."

"I don't think so. I took precautions."

"Don't underestimate your government, my friend. 'C' in Russian is pronounced like your 'S,' so first letter in CIA stands for 'sneaky.'"

This guy has a real witty sense of humor.

Robert couldn't help but grin. It probably did stand for sneaky.

"I know you don't want them to know where you are, so I arranged for you to rent apartment from my friend."

"That means your people will know where I am."

Lyosha laughed. "Of course they will. They have to. We know where all foreigners are. It is law."

"I get that."

"Apartment is by Bellarousky train station. Close to center."

As they sped up the ramp on the highway, Robert could see the red lights of cars piling up ahead. The driver simply opened the window and popped a little flashing light on top of the car. That allowed him to pass the slow traffic on the shoulder and when there wasn't any shoulder, people got out of their way.

The buildings began to take on a classic form, and their mass was impressive. He tried to sound out the names of the signs on the stores with his limited knowledge of the Cyrillic alphabet as the highway merged into a large, multi-lane street.

As they approached a huge white building, the driver pulled off the road.

"Bellarousky Vokzal. This your neighborhood."

They crawled through a mass of traffic circulating around the station and continued to head toward the center of the city. Lyosha pointed out a couple of fancy restaurants he said Robert could reach on foot.

"But, don't worry. I am your guide in Moscow. You will have first-class holiday."

They pulled up in front of a classic looking building constructed of granite.

"Most apartment buildings look like shit, but my friend's building was made by Stalin. Beautiful, no?"

Robert had to admit the architecture was strong but appealing. It looked like a hotel. They parked in front and met Lyosha's friend outside the lobby. He was short, balding, a little plump, and had beady eyes. He bore no resemblance to the crusher Lyosha was. Robert couldn't help thinking he looked a little like a used car dealer.

"Boab, this is Sasha. He will show you apartment. Everything is there – towels, toothpaste, coffee, milk. I come back in two hours after you have chance to clean up and relax. We go to store and pick up whatever else you need."

Robert nodded, shook Lyosha's hand, and followed Sasha into the building and into the elevator.

The one-bedroom apartment was comfortable and adequate for Robert's needs. Sasha showed him around, but most of it was self-explanatory. There was nothing to sign, the only papers involved were cash bills. Robert hadn't exchanged any of his currency for rubles, but, with the ruble in a freefall, Sasha was more than happy to take dollars.

After Sasha left, Robert made a cursory sweep of the apartment for bugs. Miraculously, there weren't any.

***

Lyosha picked Robert up as agreed two hours later and took him to *Tzum*, the shopping mall in the center of town where the prices were as shocking as the styles chic.

"This place expensive, but you can get anything you want here."

With the help of an attractive salesgirl, Robert stocked up on the wardrobe he would need for the week. Lyosha pushed him gently in the direction of sports jackets.

"Hey, Mr. *Noll Noll Sem*. You need to dress like secret agent for girls."

Robert shrugged. *Why not? I've got lots of cash.* He never really went out for entertainment. Whenever he wasn't on the job it was always just him and the dog. "Sounds good. What is *Noll Noll Sem*?"

"Double-oh-seven."

Robert laughed.

Lyosha sought the advice of the salesgirl who set Robert up styling. She looked at Robert and, without asking his size, took a sleek dinner jacket off the rack, slipped it over Robert's hefty shoulders and smoothed her hands over it, checking the fit against his skin. She smiled when she ran her fingers over his ample biceps. Lyosha noticed, and raised his eyebrows.

"You see? Chicks know what chicks want to see."

After giving the shopping bags to the driver, Lyosha and Robert set out on foot, past Teatralnaya Square and the majestic Bolshoi Theatre, then crossed under the busy boulevard, past the classic Hotel Metropol and the new Four Seasons, to the outskirts of the Kremlin, and entered Red Square. Dusk had fallen into darkness, which, in Moscow in the summer meant a cobalt blue sky, completely clear of clouds. As Robert entered the square, thousands of individual lights lit up the classic *GUM* shopping center building on his left like a case full of diamonds. Lenin's tomb and the castle walls of the Kremlin were on his right. The illuminated, bonfire-like, multi-colored spires of St. Basil's Cathedral were directly ahead of him. Robert stood in the middle of the square, in awe of the beauty, the history, and the power of it all.

As they walked toward the mutated towers of the 16th century cathedral, he imagined the scenes he had learned in military history of Russian forces parading into Red Square to celebrate the anniversary of the Russian Revolution, saluting as they passed by Stalin and all the highest officials of the Russian government, who were seated in the booth just to his right, and continuing on from the parade directly to the front to fight the Nazis, many of them marching for the last time of their lives. They paused in front of a circular structure near the cathedral.

"*Lubnoe mesta*. This where czar chopped off heads of his enemies."

Robert could visualize the execution of the Streltsy, the Royal Guards, who had betrayed Peter the Great. He followed Lyosha's lead, between the cathedral and the massive corner tower clock that has signaled the first minute of the New Year for every Russian for the last four-hundred years.

They continued onto a bridge across the Moscow River. When they were halfway, Robert paused at the rail, looking at battlements of the Kremlin on his right, its golden domed churches and five palaces, including the white and gold trimmed Grand Kremlin Palace, the equivalent of the White House in Russia, all lit up in their splendor.

"Beautiful, isn't it?"

"Yes."

"You will have lot of time here in day. Now party time. Even killers need holiday."

Robert was ready for party time. This place was a welcome respite from the dust, grit, grime and blood of Syria.

CHAPTER SIX

The car pulled up in front of a run down, dirty looking apartment building in the outskirts of Moscow. In fact, everywhere Robert looked there were run down, dirty looking apartment buildings. It was a stark contrast to the center of town, where all the buildings were in the classic style and beautifully maintained. They parked in a space next to rows of makeshift garages and storage units of various shapes and sizes, most of them made out of aluminum or wood with metal siding.

"We're here!"

"Where exactly are we?"

"We visit my parents."

Robert stepped out of the car and walked with Lyosha across a kid's playground, with various jungle gym equipment, swings, and painted sculptures made from old tires. There were a few kids swinging on the swings and others running around, laughing, playing what looked like hide and seek. A couple of smaller kids teetered on the seesaw.

"This where I played when I was kid. "

Robert smiled at him. "You?"

"Yeah, I used to be kid, just like you. See over there?" Lyosha pointed to an area between the buildings where there were a clump of birch trees.

"Yeah."

"That where I had first kiss. Her name was Tonya."

"You little devil. How old were you?"

"Twelve years."

They walked up a few steps to Door No. 2, rang the buzzer and the door buzzed open shortly thereafter. Upon entering, the stairwell was just about as run down and ugly as the outside of the building. It had a stale smell, like old gym socks.

"Your friend's apartment is in a lot better shape."

They began trudging up the stairs.

"He lives in center, in Stalin building. These buildings were made after war by Khrushchev. Supposed to be temporary." He laughed. "Temporary for seventy years."

On the third floor, the heavenly smell of down-home cooking filled the landing. The door of one of the four apartments was a crack open and Lyosha pushed it and ushered Robert in first. He pointed down at the floor.

"We take off shoes."

Robert and Lyosha both slipped off their shoes as a woman entered the foyer and grabbed Lyosha in a bear hug. He kissed her and she put her hands around his face, smiled and said something to him in Russian. He turned to Robert.

"Boab, this my mother, Lyudmila."

"Pleased to meet you." Robert put out his hand and she shook it.

"She don't speak English." Lyosha translated his greeting to her, although it was universally understood. A big strapping man with greying hair entered with a smile larger than the room. Robert guessed this must be Lyosha's father. They hugged in a manly way that Robert thought each one would be crushed.

"This my father, Sergei."

Sergei took Robert's hand in the same type of Vulcan death grip handshake he had experienced with Lyosha.

"It's good to meet you, sir. Thank you for having me."

The inside of the apartment was warm, cozy and clean and the heavenly scents wafting out of the kitchen were making Robert's stomach growl. Lyosha's mother gently pushed him into the bathroom, saying something to him he couldn't understand.

"She wants you to wash hands."

Lyudmila shook a towel in front of Robert and hung it back on a hook on the wall so he could see where to dry them. He washed his hands, after which Lyosha did the same.

Lyosha ushered Robert into the living room, where a dining table had been set up in the middle of the room, draped with a fine linen tablecloth and set with crystal and fine china. It was loaded with salads of all types: beet root; potato salad; fresh tomatoes and cucumbers; potatoes; smoked white and red fish; caviar; and, of course, a large plate of pickled cucumbers. Lyosha's mother was hauling in two more plates of food.

"Sit down. Eat!"

`Robert could not help but notice there were more than four place settings at the table.

"Do you have brothers and sisters coming?"

"I'm only child. Mom has sister, so aunt and cousins are coming."

Robert looked about the room, which contained the history of Lyosha's family. Photographs of people, some in black and white, adorned the buffet and the shelves of an old wooden bookcase, sagging with leather and cloth-bound books with bindings worn, indicating generations of reading. Sheer white curtains trimmed with gold covered the window and glass door leading to a balcony.

The doorbell buzzed and, before long, all the seats at the table were filled with Lyosha's aunt and uncle, a tall, skinny man, their daughter, an attractive brunette with dark hair cut straight across the forehead in bangs, and their daughter's daughter, a cute little girl of about eight years old.

Robert was the center of attention and received most of it. Lyosha's mother loaded his plate full of salads and buttered bread with red caviar. Every time Robert had finished, she reloaded his plate with the next course. First fish, then beef. Robert was beginning to feel bloated. In between plates, there was the toasting, which seemed like it would never end. Lyosha sat next to Robert and translated for him. His father stood, poured everyone's glass to the top, then remained standing, raising his glass.

"To our new American friend. Welcome to our country, our city, and our home. It is an honor to have you with us."

All eyes were on Robert as he downed his shot of vodka, then reached for a pickle. Lyosha's father spoke again, and they all looked at Robert and laughed.

"What are they laughing about?"

"They asked what you do for job. I told them you were killer." He slapped him on the back and laughed.

Lyosha's uncle Valodya, the tall, skinny fellow with the grey hair and moustache and a contagious guttural laugh, told a joke. Of course, Robert didn't understand it, but Valodya belted out laughing and Robert laughed along with everyone else. He had never remembered eating this much since he was last invited to a friend's Thanksgiving dinner about ten years ago.

As the drinking continued, so did the discussions. Robert's new friends were anxious to hear his impressions about Russia and to discuss theirs about the United States, which to Robert's surprise, were generally favorable. He could see that drinking and conversation were inexorably intertwined and one did not occur without the other. They were honest with their conversation, but he got the general impression they liked Americans and were happy to have him at their table.

Several hours into the event, the group started singing, while Lyosha's mother and aunt cleared the table. Lyosha translated for his mother.

"Mom says dinner finished. She says good for health to leave table a little hungry."

Robert nodded. It made sense, although his vodka consumption couldn't be good for health at all.

No sooner had his mother made that declaration when she and Lyosha's aunt brought in two tubs of chocolate and vanilla ice cream and a homemade cake. Sergei fetched a big bowl of candy out of the closet and set it on the table. The women retreated to the kitchen.

"I thought she said it was good for the health to leave the table hungry."

"You haven't left table yet. Now she says time for tea."

They brought in a large teapot and filled everyone's porcelain cup with tea. The time became a blur as Robert chimed in singing songs and listened to translated stories and jokes. As the time spun, so did the room around Robert's head as he took in his share of the endless flow of vodka. Finally, and maybe too late, he realized he had reached his limit and declared it.

"No more for me."

Sergei laughed and poured another round of shots, and Lyosha translated. "My father says this is last drink."

Sergei raised his glass to Robert and they drank. Robert forced another pickle down. Finally, in the early hours of morning, it was time to go. Robert said his good-byes to the aunt, uncle and cousin and to Lyosha's mother. Lyosha's niece was asleep on the couch. He looked around but didn't see Sergei.

"Where's your father?"

"Probably by door. My father is good host."

"He certainly is."

"He just wants you to feel welcome."

Robert nodded and smiled. "I do, I do."

Robert staggered to the corridor and struggled to put on his shoes, but there was still no sign of the father. Once he finally had them on, he saw Sergei standing by the door, smiling. He revealed with his hand, like a magician, three shot glasses full of vodka on the foyer table.

'Oh, no. No, no."

"*Possashok*. Drink for road. Russian tradition."

"I can't."

"My father will be insulted if you don't."

Robert squinted at the glasses, then back at Sergei, who was grinning. He took his glass, which seemed to be very heavy, and lifted it, toasted Sergei and slammed it down. Everybody shouted hooray like it was some kind of grand event, and then Robert and Lyosha stumbled out the door.

Robert, the only child of a career soldier who had taken a Lebanese wife, had long since lost both his parents. After that, the Army had been his family, and the only type of family bonds he had felt had been to the men and women he had served with. This had gotten him into some trouble the first time he had tried to walk away from this life and build a "normal" one for himself. Robert had established an "ordinary" life in New York, with a new identity, a regular job, and even had a woman in his life. But, when a fellow soldier facing a bum rap needed help, Robert had given it all up and come out from the cold to come to his aid. This type of family reunion was foreign to him, but it felt good. And even though he and Lyosha were on different "sides" he felt that comradery with him that he had felt with his fellow soldiers. It felt good to be part of something that was bigger than himself.

CHAPTER SEVEN

When Robert opened his eyes, his head was pounding. He looked at the clock. *Two thirty!*

He could see this was the way it was done in Moscow. Party late, wake up late. The inside of his mouth was dry, as if it had been wiped out with a towel and blown dry with a hair dryer. He lifted his legs out of the bed and stumbled into the kitchen. He popped the top off a liter of water and gulped it down as if there were a hole in his throat. He couldn't drink enough, but he could see that there would be no talking to Lyosha without drinking; nothing profound that is.

When in Rome.

In his case, it was "when in Russia," but he didn't care because he was on vacation anyway. He decided to spend his hours after waking doing his own sightseeing. He would wait for Lyosha to call him whenever he was ready.

He set out on foot, figuring the best way to get to know a place would be to walk it. Using a tourist map provided him by his landlord, he walked toward Red Square and the Kremlin down the large Tverskaya Boulevard, which was lined with first-class hotels and fancy boutiques. It reminded him of the Champs-Élysées in Paris. He meandered off the road into pedestrian-only streets that abutted the boulevard and took lunch at one of the cafes which served Uzbeki cuisine.

Toward the end of the day, Lyosha finally called. They started their evening atop the Smolensky Prospect building in the White Rabbit dinner club, which had a 360-degree view of Moscow through its glass walls. Lyosha pulled out all the stops, ordering a platter of fresh oysters, shrimp, lobster, and black caviar.

"Is the State picking up the tab for this, too?"

"What? Don't be silly. I invite you."

Robert guessed that meant Lyosha was paying, which he had no intention of letting him do. The waiter poured their shot glasses to the top with ice cold vodka as Robert slurped down an oyster and Lyosha dabbed a glob of caviar on a piece of buttered bread.

"They say in America you guys live to work. Here in Russia, we work to live." Lyosha savored the taste in his mouth, and lifted his shot glass to Robert.

"To peace between our countries. We will always be in business, Boab, because there will always be plenty of rich guys who pay us to kill other people, but I pray to God our people won't be killing each other."

"Amen to that." Robert toasted with Lyosha and slammed down the icy hot liquid.

The check eventually came in a Russian *matroshka* doll. Robert was too slow in realizing what it was and, by the time he did, Lyosha was already popping the head off the doll, exposing the bill inside.

"Lyosha, let me get it, please."

Lyosha held the bill out of Robert's reach. "Boab, don't insult me. You are my guest."

***

The pulsating rhythms from inside vibrated their way through the outside walls of the Icon nightclub as they approached it.

They bypassed a huge line of thrill seekers, all dressed to the nines – the men in boots and the women in stiletto heels – and went in through a special VIP entrance. Inside it was as big as a football field, not counting the second story.

The main dance floor was swimming with partiers writhing about to electronic music, most of them female. Lyosha raised his voice above the din so Robert could hear him.

"I told you – more women than men in Russia. Take your pick!" He fanned his hand toward the tender crowd like a merchant exhibiting his wares.

Robert smiled and motioned for Lyosha to move on.

"I'll take my pick later."

Lyosha nodded. They paused at a chained entrance to a staircase which led to the VIP floor and the attendant opened the chain for them to enter, closed it behind them, and led them to their private table. The second floor was also popping with dancers and revelers, but these were the girls drinking out of Dom Perignon bottles and dressed in Chanel, Dior and Celine, while their men watched them from the privacy of their tables, drinking vodka or whisky and eating caviar by the bucket load. The sweet flowery and spicy smell of hookah drifted through the air from the tall nargile water pipes at every table.

Robert and Lyosha settled back on a leather couch in front of an impressive cornucopia of fruit and cheese, and took in all the action.

"You like strip dance? They have gentlemen's club on this floor."

Robert nodded. "Maybe a little later. Let's see what's going on here first."

"Good idea. I call some girls over."

Lyosha poured a shot glass of the clear icebreaker for both of them. They simultaneously took it in one gulp, followed by a pickle. He stood up.

"I'll be back."

Robert had the impression Lyosha was attempting an Arnold Schwarzenegger impression. Not that he had to; he was taller and beefier than Arnold and Robert was sure the girls would rain over him like falling flower petals when he rumbled through the dance floor.

In less than half an hour, Lyosha was back with not one, not two, but three girls – a tall blonde with blue eyes, a sleek brunette with auburn hair and crystal green eyes, and a black haired beauty with haunting grey eyes. All of them looked like models from the covers of Vogue Magazine.

He held the blonde gently by the elbow and offered her to Robert, speaking over the pulsating beat of "Uptown Funk." "Bob, this is Svetlana, but she says you can call her Lana. She speaks English. And this is Masha and Sasha. Sounds good together, huh?" He squeezed them to his sides and they giggled.

Lana sat down next to Robert while Masha and Sasha took their places on both sides of Lyosha, as if he were a Sultan being tended by his harem. The warmth of Lana's body next to him was like a drug. He tried not to stare, but it was impossible not to look at her, dressed in a silky beige dress, cut low in the front, showing off a hint of her creamy breasts. His eyes wandered from them down to her bare legs, which disappeared under the table, then back to her face.

"So, you speak English?"

Lana smiled, perfectly pearly white and straight. She leaned in close to Robert's ear to be heard, and the tickling vibration of her voice was pleasant and overwhelming. "I learn English in school." Her accent was soft and intoxicating.

"You speak well. What would you like to drink?"

"Champagne, please."

Robert waved for the waiter, but Lyosha had already taken care of that and he ordered two bottles of the bubbly, another bottle of vodka, and a specially flavored shisha for the girls to smoke. Robert concentrated on Lana. It had been some time since he had conversed with a girl who wasn't on the clock, and even longer with one who spoke English.

"Are you still in school?"

"Oh, no. I graduate last month. I work now."

"What was your degree?"

"I have degree in accounting."

"So you work as an accountant?"

"Not yet. Too many accountants, so I work now temporarily in bakery until I can find job."

Robert thought it was odd someone with an accounting degree would be working in a bakery, but he knew most Russians had undergraduate degrees and a good many had an even higher education.

The waiter arrived with a huge chrome ice bucket – more like a tub, really, which contained two bottles of Veuve Cliquot champagne and a large bottle of Imperia Vodka buried in a mountain of crushed ice. The *Kalianchik* (hookah attendant) set down a tall crystal water pipe with half a grapefruit in place of the bowl on top. As the waiter poured champagne into the girls' flutes, the Kalianchik sucked the first batch of smoke through the tube to light the tobacco. Lana and Robert were oblivious to this ceremony.

"So where in America do you live, Bob?"

"I don't live in America. I live in Paris."

"Wow, Paris! I've always wanted to visit."

"Well, you can visit me. It's only a few hours by plane from Moscow."

For Robert's part in the rest of the small talk, he couldn't reveal anything about himself, so he recited facts in his "back-stop," the history of a person who had never existed which had been hardwired into his brain.

Lana was as interesting as she was exotic. Robert drank in her smell, a combination of French milled soap mixed with a faint hint of lavender. It had been a long time since he had been in such close contact with a woman. The last time was months ago, when he had attempted to make a "normal" life for himself in Las Vegas. Robert had attempted to take control of his own life before, but he had always marched to a different beat than others, and the only place he seemed to fit in well was in the shadows with a gun in his hand. Nevertheless, he was on vacation now and allowed himself the pleasure of being with a woman who was not for rent.

Lyosha was kissing one of his new friends on her neck and meeting no resistance, and the other was still hanging on his arm, sipping champagne. Robert couldn't understand their conversation, but it looked like he was trying to talk at least one, if not both of them, into coming home with him. It seemed he was good at more than just shooting people – persuasion was also one of his skills. No doubt it could be as useful on the battlefield as it was on the couch. Lyosha's girls eventually got up to dance to Sia's "Elastic Heart," and proved to be more supple and pliant than the music as Lyosha watched them.

As it was nearing 3 a.m., Sasha had already left and it had become clear the green-eyed Masha would be spending the rest of the night with Lyosha. He leaned over to Robert and, in a loud whisper, said, "Can you make it back to apartment on your own?"

"Yeah, yeah, no problem."

"Or maybe Svetlana can help you?" He winked. "We continue your Moscow tour tomorrow, okay?"

"Of course, go ahead, have fun."

He winked again at Robert, and he and his new partner said their good-byes to Lana.

Now Robert and Lana were completely alone. If she had been one of his targets, she wouldn't have had a chance, but this was more of a delicate pursuit. They toasted the last two glasses of champagne and Lana was the first to re-break the ice.

"Should I call us a taxi?"

Robert's brows raised. "Yes, sure."

"Taxi can drop me off at my apartment and then you at yours."

It was evident to Robert that Lana the accountant/baker was not going to be an easy first date.

"Sounds good."

The taxi ride to Lana's place was short, taken up by the essential conversation of exchanging telephone numbers. Robert's, of course, was a burner. She lived outside the centermost concentric circle of Moscow. When the taxi stopped, Robert attempted to kiss her goodnight, and she moved her neck away, but then returned to place a peck on his cheek. She slid off the taxi seat and bent in front of the open door. He tried not to stare at her cleavage.

"Good night, Bob. It was good to meet you."

"You, too. Can I call you?"

"Of course. I look forward to it."

The door closed and Robert was left with the lingering scent of Lana in the back of the taxi.

CHAPTER EIGHT

The kids were mashing their cake with their forks as their mother cleared the table. Ted Barnard was just wrapping up a dinner with his family when his cell phone rang. His wife frowned. Ted was always at work, 24 hours a day. He answered the phone.

"Yes?"

"You asked me to call you whether there were any new developments on PAL or not, sir."

Barnard rose, put down his napkin, excused himself from the table, hurried into his den and closed the door. The walls were covered with dark wood panel, the backdrop of framed photographs containing duplicate copies of himself, smiling and shaking with various presidents. He put the phone back to his ear and sat down behind his heavy wooden desk.

"What have you got?"

"That's just it, sir. Nothing. We've checked with all the hotels in Moscow, and he's not registered."

"Maybe he's staying with someone else, in their room?"

"He'd still have to register his passport. All visitors have to register with the police within 10 days."

Barnard gritted his teeth. "That means he could be off the radar for *ten days*? That's not acceptable. I want him located – now."

"Yes, sir."

"Put all our local guys on it."

"They're already looking for him, sir."

"Well, tell them to look harder!"

He disconnected and threw his phone on the desk.

***

As Robert was waking up around 11 a.m., his burner phone went off. He grabbed for it on the nightstand, expecting to hear a groggy Lyosha calling for a rain check on the continuation of Robert's Moscow tour. Instead, the first voice he heard while still lounging in his bed was the sweet accented speech of lovely Lana.

"Good morning. Did I wake you?"

"No, no, I was just getting up. I'm glad you called."

There was an awkward pause on her end. "You are? I just wanted to thank you for last evening. I had a wonderful time."

"Me, too."

Another pause, as if she couldn't think of what to say next or didn't have the nerve.

"Are you meeting with your friend today?"

"I think he'll be sleeping most of the day. Probably tonight."

"I thought so. Moscow life starts at about midnight."

"That means I must be free for lunch. Would you like to join me?"

"With pleasure, but...where?"

"I'm the stranger in town. You tell me."

"What would you like? Moscow has something for every taste."

"Well, as my guide will probably be in bed all day, I'd like to continue my tour of the city, that is, if you're willing."

"Yes, of course. In that case, there's a small café right on Red Square. It's expensive, but good. Is that okay?"

"Sure."

"I can meet you there in an hour. It's called *Bosco*. It's the only café on the square, so you can't miss it."

"Great. I'll see you there."

Robert called Lyosha's phone, which was turned off as he had expected, and left a message. Then, he got up, showered and shaved, and made some coffee in his little kitchen. Luckily, the salesgirl at Tzum had set him up with the perfect daytime wardrobe, which he slipped into and then followed the instructions Lyosha had given him to book a taxi online with the Yandex app he had downloaded on his burner phone.

The taxi pulled up as far as it could, and Robert had to walk the rest of the way to the dark stone paved square, which was closed to traffic. Even in the daylight it looked beautiful. He walked alongside the GUM shopping center building which bordered the famous plaza, and almost ran into Svetlana.

She was seated at one of several tables on the sidewalk facing the Kremlin, dressed in a flowery blouse with a silk scarf around her neck fluttering in the warm breeze, and she waved to Robert when she saw him approach. He pulled up a chair and sat down next to her.

"Hello, Lana. You were right. This place was easy to find."

She smiled. She was even more stunning in the light of day. "I ordered us some mineral water and I asked for menus in English."

"Great." Robert picked up the menu, but was distracted from reading it while he took in her beauty.

"They even have a hamburger."

"That's for back home. What do you suggest?"

"Well, since you are in Russia, why not a traditional Russian dish, like Beef Stroganoff? And you could pair it with some homemade pickles."

"I've had my share of pickles the last two days, but the Beef Stroganoff sounds good."

"Then maybe you should have some Olivier salad. That way you have two traditional Russian foods both designed by French chefs."

"Really?" To Robert and to most everyone else he knew, Russia had always been an anomaly. Here they were, in the center of the city that had burned down around Napoleon's army, having "traditional" Russian cuisine that had been invented by the French.

As they relaxed and got to know each other better, Robert discovered that Lana had him committed for the entire afternoon.

"I thought after lunch we could visit the Kremlin."

Robert's eyes raised to hers. "The Kremlin?"

"The Armory Museum and churches. Every visitor should see them. Then we can finish the day with a walk around the Novodevichy Convent."

"Isn't that where the czars banished their wives and female relatives?"

Lana laughed. "Yes, but the grounds are beautiful despite their gloomy historical significance."

While Robert was sipping tea and drinking in his new company, an obscure tourist who was mulling along with the crowd of gawkers in the square, put his phone to his ear.

"I have him."

"*Where is he?*"

"Central Moscow."

"Good. Keep an eye on him but don't be seen. And don't engage him unless you're engaged."

The stranger clicked off, wandered over to the café, and took a seat at the farthest table from Robert and Lana. He was dressed in the standard American tourist uniform: T-shirt and jeans with a baseball hat and a light grey windbreaker – the latter being his own fashion statement. He ordered a cup of coffee and sipped on it while he was waiting for them to get their check and pay. When they got up and walked toward the Kremlin, he threw some cash on the table and stood.

***

After almost two hours, Robert had seen his fair share of churches and Fabergé eggs and was ready to leave the Kremlin Armory Museum until they came upon the arms collection. The massive collection contained weapons dating back to the 11th Century. He entered the hall and was held captive, fascinated by the 17th Century firearms created by the masters of Russian gunsmiths. He leaned over the case containing a pair of shiny Dutch Wheelock pistols on which heads had been delicately carved into their ivory handles. Robert stared at them as though they were the most beautiful things he had ever seen. He pictured two stubborn land barons, facing each other off over a duel because of some drunken argument or insult, and became lost in that moment of history.

"Are you alright?"

He suddenly became aware again of her presence.

"Oh, yeah, yeah."

"It seems you like guns."

Robert smiled. "They're beautiful."

Lana hooked her arm into his elbow and admired the pistols. "Yes, for something so destructive, their beauty is ironic. I wonder if they've ever killed anybody."

Robert was pondering the same. "Probably not. They look ceremonial, and if they were a gift to the czar, he probably didn't shoot anyone with them."

"I don't know. Czars were killers, you know."

It was paradoxical to Robert to think he was enjoying the company of someone who would be repulsed if she knew who he truly was. And she was oblivious to it.

After an hour in the true armory of the museum, Lana was getting sick of looking at guns and Robert had had enough of the Kremlin, so she suggested they move on. As they exited the battlements of the fortress, a lone man stood in the crowd, unnoticed by them and by everyone. But he was aware of them. It was his obligation.

CHAPTER NINE

The sun gleamed off the white walls of the Novidevichy Convent, sparkled on the surface of the Moscow River and lit up the brilliant gold leaf onion-domed roofs of the convent's church. Robert was uneasy. Because it had been so long since he had really relaxed, he had dropped his guard, and he was now chiding himself for it. In Robert's business, as in his life, failing to be vigilant meant simply that you were dead. His lack of attention to his surroundings and dedication of their observance to only his peripherals was putting him at risk, and this was the cause of his angst. For Robert, being out in open spaces like this only meant one thing – he was a potential target.

He turned to Lana, who was watching some kids throw pieces of bread to the ducks from the bank of the river.

"Lana, this place is beautiful, but maybe we can go where we can sit down, have some coffee."

"Okay. I'm kind of tired after all that walking in the Kremlin anyway. But we can sit down here. It's very pleasant." She pointed to a bench by the river.

"Well, I'm kind of thirsty."

Robert's unrest only honed his usually acute senses to alert himself to everything in his surroundings – the kids feeding ducks, mothers rolling their babies in carriages – gardeners tending to flower beds. And then he saw him. The stranger looked out of place, an artist's mistaken stroke on the canvas. The man in the grey windbreaker was trying to blend in, but it wasn't working for him. Robert took the lead, taking Lana by her arm. She was surprised, at the same time pleased by the gesture, but Robert had not intended it to be an affectionate one.

He increased their pace, surreptitiously watching the adventitious wanderer. They slipped behind a hedge in the garden. The move made Lana anticipate a kiss was in the making, but he surprised her by asking for a taxi instead.

"Okay, I'll order one."

She punched in the order for the taxi on her smartphone and, when she had finished, Robert whisked them away, noting that the interloper had just casually passed them.

Typical surveillance move. Everything in plain sight.

Robert had tried to get a good look at his face, but it proved to be problematical because he couldn't look at him straight on. However, he took a mental snapshot that would have been good enough to identify a suspect in any lineup. Lana looked at her smartphone.

"The taxi is here. Yellow cab, number 370."

"Good."

Robert ushered her to the main parking lot. There he saw the stranger getting into a white Lada.

He's using a Russian car.

As they rode, he speculated who could be watching him. Was it Lyosha's people, who certainly had the right, or was it his own? Or was it some unknown faction which an interest in Robert's deadly activities? It was a question that must be answered, otherwise Robert would never have peace. He always needed to know who was friend or foe, and it was an ever changing dynamic that needed constant observation and reflection. He kept looking through the back window, and Lana could sense he was worried about something.

"You know, I should probably check in with Lyosha. Do you mind if we take a rain check on that cup of coffee?"

"No, no, that's fine. I'll tell the taxi driver to take me home."

They sat in silence as they rode toward her apartment in the outskirts of the city. As they slowed to drop Lana off, Robert asked her, "How do you say 'wait' in Russian?"

She smiled. "*Padazhdite*. If you were asking someone to wait for you, you would say, '*Padazhdite pajalousta*' which means 'wait please.'"

Robert gave her a hug and bid her farewell, leaving her with a questioning expression and lingering question, which she was brave enough to ask.

"Will we see each other tonight?"

Robert was preoccupied, which she may have interpreted as ambivalence or uncertainty.

"Oh, yes, yes. I'll call you later."

She smiled, shut the door and turned to go into her apartment. The taxi driver pulled away from the curb and down the street.

"*Padazhdite, pajaoulsta.*"

The driver stopped, amused. He had heard them speaking English and now the foreigner was taking his travel Russian for a test drive. Robert looked through the driver's side mirror at the white Lada, which had left Lana's apartment building, but then had stopped when they had.

Could he be even more obvious?

"Okay." Robert motioned the driver with animated hands and he accelerated, heading toward the center of town.

When Robert began to recognize the landmarks on Tverskaya Street, he told the driver to let him out there.

"Can you stop here please? Stop, stop."

The driver obliged, turning right into a side street and stopping there. It was almost impossible to pull over on the hectic boulevard at such a busy time. Every lane was filled with cars, speeding by as if they were on a highway. As Robert paid, he noticed the white Lada had stopped a block ahead of them. It was time for Robert to make his move, and fast. He exited the car, and walked quickly to an underground crossing, slipping into it just as he noticed the stranger in the grey windbreaker picking up his pace to a sprint.

Now that the stranger couldn't see him, Robert ran as fast as he could through the underground passage to the other side of the busy thoroughfare. Once there, he leaped up the stairs three at a time and blended into a crowd of people on the street, looking back over his shoulder. His pursuer was there, but searching around like a rat sniffing for a missing piece of cheese. Robert surfed the crowd until he got to the corner and took a quick right toward the railway station. This was close to his neighborhood and he had memorized all of the surroundings.

Using traditional counter-surveillance measures, Robert doubled back and checked behind him as he traversed the street. No sign of the mysterious stranger. He ducked into another side street and was finally on the block of his apartment. He scanned everyone in the area, and, convinced that the stranger was not among them, flashed his security key at the door to the building and it buzzed open.

When he had finally shut the door of the apartment behind him, Robert looked through the drapes of the living room window onto the street below. Everything looked as normal as one would expect it to be. For now.

CHAPTER TEN

The more he thought about it, the more insecure he became. He outlined his options to himself. For one thing, he didn't know who was following him, whether ally or enemy. That unknown variable had to be uncovered in order to determine an appropriate course of action, whether it be to evade, ignore or eliminate the potential obstacle. He made up his mind there was only one way to do that – he had to confront the sycophant face to face.

Lyosha did check in with Robert by early evening and sounded as though he had just crawled out of bed. He proposed that Robert meet him at Pushkin Café for a late dinner around 11 p.m.

Lana was right about Moscow night life.

Until he had identified the stalker, Robert didn't want to involve Lana. To compromise her safety just to be in her company would be selfish, but, above all, it would shave off his edge, and that edge was something he very much needed to have to resolve the problem. He dialed her number and she answered on the first ring.

"Hi Lana, it's Bob."

"Hi, Bob, I knew it was you. Is everything alright?"

"Oh, yeah, fine, fine. I wanted to let you know that Lyosha just made a meeting with me for tonight so I'm not going to be free."

There was silence on the end. Then, "I see."

"But I'd like to see you tomorrow if that's alright. Not only are you a terrific tour guide, but you're also wonderful company."

Her voice brightened up. "I would love to."

"Good. I'll call you tomorrow, say around 11?"

"Sure, I look forward to it."

Robert said his good-byes and began to craft a strategy in his mind. Without giving away his location, he would have to offer himself as bait. To do that, he decided to start where he had lost his obsequious chaser and backtrack to cover all the public places where he may be lurking to pick up Robert's trail.

At about 10:00 p.m., Robert set his plan into motion. He surreptitiously made a convoluted path to the underground passageway where he had lost the stalker and crossed under Tverskaya Street. There, he openly strolled the boulevard all the way down to Red Square, stopping to look in the store windows along the way. All the while, he was mindful of his surroundings, always on the lookout for his mysterious pursuer.

Robert sauntered through the entrance to the famous square and wandered around before stopping for a cup of coffee at Bosco. While he sipped, he watched the passers-by and scanned the area for the stranger.

Nothing.

He knew that he was a target for surveillance and, if this stalker was a professional like him, he would not have given up after he had lost track of Robert. Moreover, he would do his best not to be seen himself.

He's out there, somewhere lurking in the shadows. I can feel him.

Robert finished his coffee and settled his bill, then proceeded past St. Basil's Cathedral, out of the square and across the bridge over the Moscow River. He stood there looking out over the rail at the massive battlements of the Kremlin and the huge gold onion dome of the Christ the Savior Cathedral perched on the banks of the river. He checked his watch.

10:40. He has to have seen me by now.

Whether he had or not, Robert had to run to Pushkin Square to meet Lyosha. He set out back through Red Square, out the Voskresensky gates and through the underground passage under Okhotnyy Ryad Street to Tverskaya. When he arrived to Pushkin Café he was about 15 minutes late.

He checked in with the maître d', who showed him to Lyosha's table on the first floor. Lyosha stood up and shook his hand vigorously.

"Hello, my friend. I thought you were lost."

"No, no, was just doing some sightseeing in Red Square. It's quite a walk from there."

The maître d' pulled out a chair for Robert and Lyosha sat as Robert lowered himself into it.

"You can take metro. In five minutes you're here."

Robert smiled, and kept the secret of his mission to himself. "Can't do much sightseeing underground."

"Oh, that's where you're wrong, my friend. The metro stations are very beautiful. Some tour guides charge to show you best ones. I will do it – and for free!"

"I appreciate that."

***

Pushkin Café was styled in the 18th Century time of its namesake, Alexander Pushkin, the famous Russian poet. The walls were wood paneling and carved ceilings, and bookcases filled with antique, leather bound books. Robert could see this was going to be another long dinner with a lot of drinking, for which he had tempered himself so he could keep his senses.

"What's wrong, my friend? Have you had enough vodka for one holiday?"

"No, I'm fine, just trying to save myself from a hangover."

"You were sick next morning?"

Robert hated to play the weakling.

"No, I just have to get up earlier tomorrow. I have a date."

"A date! With Svetlana, I bet."

Robert nodded. "You've caught me!"

"You filthy bastard! Of course! Tonight, you are officially excused from drinking!"

What Robert did do was excuse himself from the table to go to the restroom and to place a call to Lana. Instead, he bypassed the bathroom break and went outside to play the part of a duck in a shooting range. It worked. Within seconds of exiting the restaurant, Robert spotted his stalker, this time dressed in a plain T-shirt, trying to blend in with the droves of humanity in the greenbelt across the street. Robert bummed a cigarette and a light from the doorman, shuttled down the stairs, turned to his right, and slowly wandered into an alley, where he pretended to smoke it, and kept walking. From a casual glance over his shoulder, he could see the stalker trotting across the street, tailing him. Robert chucked the cigarette, ducked behind some garbage cans, and waited.

The stalker ran into the alley and looked around in a panic, hunting for Robert, who remained patiently crouched. Just as the stranger began to pass the trash cans, Robert burst out from them, pushed into the man with his hand against his throat, disarmed him in a flash, smashed him against the opposite wall, and held his own gun under his chin. The man, who appeared to be an American, white, brown-haired, about 35, was shivering with fear. It was obvious to Robert he knew who he was following.

"Turn around asshole."

Robert forced him around, pushed the barrel of the gun to the back of his neck and smashed his nose into the wall as he frisked him with his free hand. Robert knew every conceivable place to hide a gun and searched in all those areas. He found a small .22 in a hidden holster under the man's belt.

"I can see you know who I am. Now who the hell are you and who are you working for?"

"I'm with the company."

Robert deprived the man of his wallet and cell phone, and he pocketed the phone and held onto the wallet.

"You're pretty shitty for a ghost. Can you prove you're with the company?"

"You know I can't."

"Who do you report to?"

"The Deputy Director for Operations."

"The man with no name."

"Yes."

Robert was furious. He pulled out the contents of the man's wallet and went through them like a deck of playing cards, discarding each credit card and dropping them on the ground as if he were dealing them.

"Where's your passport? Your registration?"

"Not there."

"Obviously. What's your name?'

"You know I'm not..."

Robert turned him, grabbed him by the throat and shoved the gun under his chin. "I asked you a question. You have exactly three seconds to answer it. Your name – the name your parents gave you. One..."

The man was trembling.

"Two..."

"David. David Gunther."

"Now you listen to me, David Gunther. If I see you or any of your buddies stalking me again it won't go as well for you next time. Got it?"

"Yes, yes." Sweat had beaded on Gunther's head and was dripping into his right eye, which he was blinking. Robert pocketed the guns and threw the wallet at the man's feet.

"Now get the hell out of here!"

The man nodded and crouched to pick up his wallet and the contents.

"I said now!"

He swept them up in his hands, shoved them into his pockets and ran off.

CHAPTER ELEVEN

Robert's evening with Lyosha had to come to an early end. After fighting over who was going to pay the bill (and losing), he begged his leave.

"You can't possibly have something better to do than what I have planned for you."

Robert didn't respond. He just smiled.

"You filthy bastard! I know what you're planning to do!"

Lyosha offered Robert a ride, but the last thing he wanted was to be trailed to his apartment. So he feigned an excuse that he was going to meet Lana there at Pushkin Café. Lyosha accepted it on its face, eloquently, holding onto Robert's hand a little longer after the shake and looking directly into his eyes. He sensed the reason for Robert's early departure from the evening's festivities was not just to meet a girl.

"I have a feeling my friend is cutting his Russian holiday short."

Robert nodded. "I think I have to."

"Trouble back home?'

"Something like that."

Robert didn't tell him the "trouble back home" had followed him to Moscow.

"You need ride to airport?"

"No, that wouldn't work. I have to disappear."

"Understood. Leave keys in apartment and just close door. My friend will collect them tomorrow afternoon."

"Thank you, Lyosha, for everything."

"You're welcome, *Noll-noll-sem*. You have memorized my PGP key?"

"Yes."

"Good. Let's stay in touch. You know, for American, you are pretty good guy."

"And for a Russian, you're a pretty good guy yourself."

Lyosha gave Robert a shoulder hug, Robert latched onto his shoulder and slapped it, and then Lyosha took off on his way. Robert had a cup of coffee while he waited for an appropriate time to pass. Then, his phone rang. It could only be one of two people, and one had just left.

"Hello Lana."

"How did you know it was me?"

"Only two people have this number."

"Oh. I just wanted to make arrangements for the continuation of your city tour tomorrow." She was upbeat and sounded excited.

"Lana, I don't think I'll be able to make it tomorrow. "

"Can I ask why?"

"I really can't explain it over the phone."

There was another awkward moment of silence. Then, "I understand." Her voice was deflated.

Robert felt bad that he couldn't see her. After all, he had invested his time with her and did enjoy her presence. But, in his world, everything was temporary and the momentary thing that counted above all else was his life.

"I'm sorry. Can I call you sometime?"

"Sure, Bob, you can call."

Robert disconnected and pulled the alleged David Gunther's phone out of his pocket. It was a cheap burner phone, just like his. He examined the recent calls, but none of them looked familiar. He rang the last number that had called Gunther, listened quietly and heard a male voice on the other end.

"You have eyes on the rabbit?"

A "rabbit" was spy talk for someone they were following. Robert felt relief that he had heard rabbit and not "target."

"Is this the man with no name?"

"Who are you?"

"This is the rabbit."

A pause, then, "Is the officer with you?"

"I sent him home. Don't worry, he's okay. I don't take kindly to being followed though, especially after you fucked up the pickup. This is pretty sloppy work."

"Come in and we'll talk about it."

"I'm on vacation. You authorized it. I'll come in when it's over."

Robert clicked off the phone, left it on the radiator next to the table, and got up to leave.

***

In the cloak room, Robert approached another American man who was putting on a light coat over his shoulders and a hat on his balding head.

"Hey, buddy, I'll give you a grand if you trade your coat and hat for my leather jacket."

The man looked at Robert as if he had just asked to swap wives.

"What?"

"My jacket and a thousand bucks for your coat and hat. Can't beat that for a deal."

"Uh, no thanks. I'm not interested." The man straightened his coat, turned away and started to button it.

Robert got in front of and very close to the man and, in a low tone, said, "I didn't ask if you were interested. I'll make it fifteen hundred."

Robert took off his leather jacket and dove into his pocket for the cash. He handed both to the man, who just looked down at the money and back up at Robert.

"Come on." He shook the jacket and money in front of his face.

The man reluctantly took the money first and shoved it into his pants pocket, then removed his coat and hat and gave them to Robert. Then, with a strange look, he snatched the jacket from Robert's hand. Robert left without giving it a second thought, pulling the duster over his shoulders and covering his head with the hat. He waited at the exit for a group of French tourists to leave and pretended he was going with them, tagging along with his head down and hat hiding his features. When they piled into a waiting car, he opened the door of the taxi behind them. The driver looked over his shoulder into the backseat.

"*Bellarousky Vakzal.*"

The driver shook his head. "*Ya zanit.*"

Robert figured that must mean he was waiting on a reservation, so he had to be forceful and convincing.

"*Bellarousky Vakzal*," Robert repeated, and handed the driver a crisp one-hundred dollar bill. The driver's eyes opened wide and he took it without hesitation, unlike the American guy with the coat and hat, and pulled away from the curb immediately.

When he was dropped off at the Bellarousky train station, he went into the main entrance in an inflow of people, and retreated into the restroom. He checked into an empty stall and locked the door. Then, he released the clips on both the guns and cracked the slides, popping the rounds out of the chamber. He emptied the magazines into his coat pocket. He broke down the .22 and then the 9mm, taking out the slides, recoil springs, barrels, strikers and plungers, extractors and safety pins, and mixed them all together in the other pocket of the coat. He exited the restroom and then out of the station on a wave of people leaving. Using his counter-surveillance techniques, he made his way back to the apartment, dropping the bullets in one trash can and scattering the gun components randomly in five separate cans along the way.

There was no time to waste. He knew who was following him but he didn't know why. He had to leave for the airport immediately. On home ground he could sort it out more efficiently and easily. He packed the things he had purchased during his short stay in Moscow into his knapsack. Instead of ordering a taxi, he would walk back to the station and take the Aeroexpress train to the airport. He threw the keys on the entry table, pulled the door shut behind him and it clicked into place.

Robert slung his pack over his shoulder and double-timed it to the train station, dumping the burner phone in a garbage receptacle along the way. He purchased a ticket in the machine for the next Aeroexpress to Sheremetyevo Airport and lay low for about 30 minutes until boarding. Like a chameleon, he mingled in with the crowd. The crowd was an international, cosmopolitan mix of people. With his swarthy skin and short black hair, he could easily pass for just about any nationality or ethnicity, whether Spanish, Italian, Arabic, or Armenian. In the hustle and bustle of the waiting area, he blended right in and then he withdrew into the shadows, which was where he had always felt the most comfortable.

The boarding announcement echoed through the station. Robert merged with the flood of people hurrying for the train, but hung back against the wall by the platform and waited until everyone had boarded. Then, just as the conductor shouted last call, he shuffled off to a car in the middle of the train and took a seat, alert to everything and everyone in his surroundings. When he was completely sure he was not being followed, he walked through the cars to the first-class cabin at the anterior of the train.

***

At the airport, Robert paid cash for the next flight to Paris on Aeroflot, which was in approximately two hours. After purchasing his ticket, he went directly through passport control and security, but he didn't enter the business class lounge until he had made a tour through the duty-free shops, just to make sure nobody was tailing him. If it was truly the CIA who was following him, they knew where he lived anyway and he would meet up with one of their agents in Paris. He could have chosen to disappear at that point, but he had tried before and it didn't work out too well, so he decided to face whatever the problem was and to do it on his own turf.

CHAPTER TWELVE

The lush green forests surrounding Moscow faded from view through the airplane portal, giving way to feathery white, misty clouds as he bade the strange and wonderful city farewell. Four hours later, he landed in a different world. Deplaning first was a luxury for business class passengers but a necessity for him, so he could make it home as soon as possible without being seen and fortify himself for any type of confrontation. Robert was known in espionage circles as an "illegal." As such, he was completely expendable and if he was ever caught, his own government would deny any responsibility or authority for his actions. This was the world in which he operated. The adage: "Keep your friends close and your enemies closer" was always at work in Robert's life, because he ran the risk of having either one of them wipe him from the face of the earth at any time.

He opted to take the RER train from the airport into central Paris. It was an efficient way to travel for someone who always had to have eyes in the back of his head. He made the brisk walk to the train station in the terminal, bought his ticket in the machine, descended the escalator to the track and caught the double-decker train. Thirty-five minutes later he was getting off at Gare du Nord and descended into the metro station.

He took the subway to the Michel-Ange stop in the 16th Arrondissement neighborhood of Porte d'Auteil.

He carefully made his way down Rue Erlanger to his apartment building, but, instead of his apartment, he headed first to his storage locker in the basement. The cellar was a cool, dirt-floored, musty labyrinth of storage units with wooden doors, each secured with its own padlock. Robert retrieved the key from behind a loose panel in the wall where he had hidden it and opened the brass padlock on his locker. After a few minutes of shuffling things around, he found what he was looking for under a pile of old magazines – an aluminum gun case. He flipped open the latches on the case and opened the lid to reveal a Glock 17 packed in foam with two fully loaded clips. Robert pocketed one clip, lifted the handgun out of the case, slapped in the other clip and jacked the slide. He was ready for his homecoming.

He approached the door to his apartment with caution. He inserted his key and turned it slowly and gently without making even a clicking sound, and crouched low as he pushed the portal open. He entered as if he were a police officer searching someone's house other than his own, but intimately familiar with the layout. All of the shutters were drawn closed, the way he had left him, which left the room completely dark, so the sliver of light from the opening door illuminated the entire area and, in the umbra he could see a figure seated in one of the two reclining chairs. Robert aimed his gun at the figure and yelled out.

"*Ne bouges pas*! Don 't move!"

He recognized the gruff voice from the man in the chair.

"Don't worry, Paladine. I have no intention of moving."

It was the man with no name himself.

"Why are you here? In my house?"

Robert flipped on the light, keeping his gun trained on the familiar intruder, approaching him like a cautious cop.

"I have an assignment for you."

"You know I've only got four more jobs, and then I'm outta here. A free man."

Robert smiled and the man looked at him with disgust.

"So I've heard."

"So why are *you* delivering it to me? This isn't the way it's done."

The man turned his head, locking his ice-cold eyes onto Robert's.

"It's done the way I say it's done. I'm the Deputy Director for Operations."

"Congratulations. A title so classified you can't even list it on your resumé when they fire you."

The Deputy Director did have a name, although he had never disclosed it to Robert. Robert had checked him out, although the identity of the Director of Clandestine Operations was so secret, all he was able to find was a rumor that the real name of the man standing before him was Gregory Manizek. The job of the Directorate for Operations was so dirty that it, and even the name of its director, had to be kept a secret. Robert almost laughed at Manizek's serious look because of the way he puckered his furry, Brezhnev-style eyebrows. Those and his little mouth made him look kind of like an owl.

"So what are you doing in Paris?"

"Your actions necessitated I handle the situation personally."

Where do they get A-holes like this?

"My actions?"

"Cavorting with an agent of the enemy and running off to Moscow."

"The enemy? So we're at war with Russia now?"

"Very funny. Do you want to put that gun down now?"

Manizek carefully withdrew a pack of cigarettes from his pocket and put one in his mouth.

"As soon as you put down your cigarette. No smoking."

Manizek frowned and smiled, though not from amusement. He released the unlit cigarette from his fingers and crushed it into the rug with the ball of his foot. Robert sheathed his weapon, showing no reaction to the actions of his impolite houseguest.

"Why don't you sit down, Paladine?"

Robert took a seat in the chair across from him. Between them was a coffee table and on it a plain, unmarked manila folder.

"Why do you keep calling me that?"

"You're not the only one without a name. And you earned that pseudonym yourself by acting foolishly and irresponsibly. I was against taking you back, you know."

"So was I."

"We didn't appreciate you taking off like that. You weren't following instructions."

"I didn't appreciate being chased by an army of head-chopping, jihadist thugs to a pickup zone where there was no pickup."

"If it was up to me, after that stunt you pulled in New York, I would have reactivated you, court-martialed your ass and gone for the death penalty."

"Yeah, well it wasn't up to you." Robert motioned with his head to the folder on the table. "I assume that file is what you came to deliver, so why don't you get the hell out of here before I call the cops to report a dead trespasser in my apartment?"

Manizek frowned with disgust as Robert picked up the folder. He rose his lanky body from the chair and approached within a breath of Robert's face. "Your assignment is Adnan Khalil."

Robert opened the folder and flipped through the dossier. "He lives in Paris? That's not the deal. I never do a job in my hometown." He pushed the file against Manizek's chest and let go of it.

"The deal is whatever we say it is and besides, you don't have a home." Manizek threw the folder back on the table.

Robert grinned, tried to hide his disappointment. After this job, it's true, he would again be homeless. Just as a cat won't crap where it eats, he couldn't live in a town where he had killed somebody. He latched onto Manizek's cold, steel-grey eyes. "So what's so special about this guy?"

"Why? He's your assignment. Just do it."

Robert gave Manizek a cold stare.

"Adnan Khalil is a terrorist. He's the suspected mastermind of the Charlie Hebdo attacks."

"Then he's a French problem. What does it have to do with us?"

"He's a bad guy. Maybe even worse than you. The main recruiter for ISIS in Europe. His specialty is cultivating suicide bombers – who've been blowing up American targets almost exclusively. The president himself wants this one done. He'd do it himself, but we can't send a drone after him in the heart of Paris."

"I'll take a look at it."

Manizek glared at him. "Don't question your assignment, just follow it. We own your ass and don't forget it. Every time you get a portfolio like this you're expected to execute it without hesitation."

Robert squinted his blank eyes at the man. "Then you'd better hope a dossier like this never pops up with your name in it."

Manizek smiled again and stood up to take his leave. He paused in the foyer and turned to Robert.

"This guy's under round-the-clock surveillance."

"Great. All the more reason for the French to take care of it."

"They want to put him in prison. To do that, first they have to catch him in an overt act. Who knows how many people will die in the meantime? Then it'll be years in French courts. In those years, he will have sent hundreds more of Americans to early graves. We want to send him on his way – now."

The man with no name left without saying good-bye, which was just fine with Robert. He shut the door behind him and thought to himself this would not be the last time he would see the man, and he didn't look forward to the next time.

CHAPTER THIRTEEN

Thousands of miles away, in McLean, Virginia, Nathan Anderson picked up the phone. It was his counterpart, Ted Barnard, from the CIA.

"Just wanted to give you a head's up."

"What's happening?"

"The PAL situation has been contained."

"Is he still in operation?"

"Yes, back on the job. Seems he was a little pissed off when his ride didn't show up after the last job."

"Wouldn't you be?"

"Nathan, you have to remember, this is the guy who joined a terrorist group in New York and killed a guard at the Indian Point Energy Center in the midst of a near nuclear disaster."

"Are you more embarrassed because he accomplished what nobody else in any counter-terrorism unit could or angry that he marches to the beat of his own drum?"

"Whatever. Somehow you were able to convince the president we needed him and now it is what it is."

"Well, thanks for keeping me posted."

Nathan set his phone down on the desk. It felt good to know something he had done had made a difference and he knew he was just a step away from making his agency the go-to center for combatting terrorism. Paladine was definitely the right choice and he smiled to himself with pride at having been given the credit for it.

***

Robert studied the contents of the folder to reveal his latest assignment. Adnan Khalil was a jihadist recruiter for ISIS who was credited, unofficially, with masterminding the Charlie Hebdo attack. That meant he would be on everyone's radar, all the time. It wasn't going to be a free-for-all like it was in civil war torn Syria or a hit on an obscure person that the government had on their "watch list" but wasn't really watching whom he could waste and then walk away without a witness.

This one is going to be a real challenge.

Robert secured the file away. He would memorize the details, destroy them, and keep the picture for verification. But he had to take care of more important things first – he had to get his dog.

He had dropped the dog off at a home near the Bois de Boulogne, whose owners had bragged they would treat the dog as one of their own. They were two metro stops away, in a beautiful residential area of the city that was just a few steps from the forest.

When Robert appeared at their front door, the big scruffy dog with the droopy ears howled, forced its way through the door, practically knocking him over, and assaulting him with his huge tongue. Robert kneeled down and absorbed the affection from who was probably the closest being to him on the earth.

"Hey, Butthead, how ya doin' boy?"

The lady standing at the door, a lanky 40-something with a short haircut, smiled.

"Why did you name him Butthead?'

Robert laughed. "Cause he's butt-ugly and it's almost impossible to tell his face from his rear end."

Butthead's French boarders couldn't get used to his unconventional name, but, as English was not their first language, they didn't seem to think it was that funny. It just happened to be the first thing Robert had called the dog and it stuck to him as a name. Robert thanked and paid Butthead's hosts and the two took off. The dog was so well trained, it stuck right by Robert's side – no need for a leash.

They took the long way home, across the street and through the forest. Once they were in the wild, Robert relaxed the restrictions on the dog and he romped around, smelling and watering trees and wagging his tail like a helicopter blade. They traversed the first part of the forest, which was a huge rolling lawn surrounding a large pond. The dog fell on the grass, turned on its back and writhed around like he was trying to scratch an itch he couldn't reach. Robert laughed so hard he thought he would pee his pants.

He ran toward an adjacent jogging trail at a light trot and the dog galloped dutifully behind him. The trail led them into the thick of the forest, with trees so tall the sunlight was filtered through their leaves and branches, which made an artful sky of sunrays as well as a cooling effect. Both dog and man felt in touch with nature as Robert walked along the trail and the dog meandered off a bit, sniffing his way through the labyrinth of trees and stopping to gulp water from a babbling stream.

Robert whistled, and the dog popped out from the thick expanse of forest and lumbered back onto the trail, its muzzle dripping with water, and ran to him. They wandered through the dirt trail until they came upon another clearing: A picnic area – another large expanse of grass which was about the halfway point for home. The dog was curious about the families who were picnicking on blankets they had spread out on the grass and the teenagers who were using their blankets for necking. He would have loved to have shared any kind of picnic leftovers, but knew better than to invite himself to the party. Robert dropped onto the grass and the dog jumped on top of him. They wrestled for a while. Then, they got up and headed home. There was much work to be done.

***

He spent the evening researching Khalil's patterns on social media. Like most jihadist recruiters, Khalil was active on both Facebook and Twitter, but he wasn't the type to post a "play-by-play" of his daily activities. No selfies, no pictures of his cat, no jokes. Just jihadi propaganda. From the file Manizek had given him, he had Khalil's home address. Khalil worked out of his home – there was no separate work location. He was able to pick up only a few tidbits of information from the traditional net, and then dove into the alternate Internet – the Darknet – for more in-depth research. There, the rhetoric against the infidels was stronger, but Khalil had been careful. He hadn't given away the location of any of his meetings or appointments or the details of any of his activities.

Robert began the next day surveilling Khalil. Hiding in plain sight in the periphery of the hustle and bustle of the city, he watched the terrorist leave his home in the morning. He noticed that he wasn't the only one watching, however. Plainclothes cops from who-knows-what agency were also stalking him. He first noticed their unmarked white car parked in a space on Khalil's street in the 8th Arrondissement. Only a policeman or a very persistent person could ever hope to find a parking space on the street in that busy Parisian neighborhood. One of the cops exited the white car and followed Khalil on foot. Robert carefully hung back as he casually walked in the same general direction.

Khalil stopped at the corner bakery for a croissant and a cup of coffee. Robert couldn't help but notice his Parisian habits, as well as his expensive attire. Khalil's $1,000 euro Ferragamo Python shoes were a dead giveaway

Quite the hypocrite, isn't he?

The more Robert watched Khalil rubbing elbows with the people, flirting with the bakery shop girl and smiling at everyone around him, the more he began to dislike him. But he was, after all, a salesman, selling jihad to impressionable youngsters, disillusioned teenagers desperately searching for purpose in their mundane lives. But that dream led to nothing but pain and death, for both the young people themselves and their victims. Khalil finished his breakfast and took off from the bakery at a brisk pace, ducking into the metro station, followed by the undercover dick. Robert attached himself to a crowd of commuters and scurried down the stairs after them.

He could see Khalil and the stalking policeman both ahead, already past the turnstiles and heading in the direction of the Champs Élysées. Robert hung back, passing a saxophone-playing man in the tunnel, and flowed with the commuters to the platform. He watched as the approaching train slowed to a stop, the people poured out, and Khalil stepped on. The cop also stepped on, one car down. Robert waited on the platform at the end car, observing until the final buzzer sounded the closing of the doors. He was halfway through the door when he saw Khalil suddenly come out in a brisk walk. Robert ducked out and made himself a part of the wall as he watched the detective attempt to leave as well, but the train pulled away from the track with the cop still in it and Khalil bounded up the stairs against the "do not enter" signs and across the platform to the track for the other direction. Robert doubled back around quickly and crossed the tracks as well, just as the train arrived, and jumped into the last car of the center-bound train with his eyes on Khalil at all times.

He resisted the temptation to take this window of opportunity to take out Khalil with the .22 Ruger with the noise suppressor he kept strapped to his calf. He was a professional and that meant not only the hit had to be perfect, but his getaway as well, so Robert fulfilled his original plan to observe all of his target's daily patterns. Khalil would live to die another day.

CHAPTER FOURTEEN

Robert's instincts proved to be correct when Khalil picked up another not-as-obvious tail upon exiting the Place de Clichy metro station. Whoever had him under surveillance had obviously already nailed down his daily patterns. He stayed behind and followed the tail as he stalked Khalil. Beyond the respectable centerpiece of the square were row upon row of sex shops and erotic supermarkets offering products, films, and live shows catering to any prurient taste. Khalil headed off the beaten path toward that area, where the more intimate entertainment could be had.

Nice start for a morning. Breakfast of champions.

Khalil passed a row of sleazy storefronts and paused to look at one. A scantily clad young woman sauntered out and attempted to lure him in, but he refused her advances and kept walking. Finally, at the corner, he darted into one of the shops and his follower stood outside at a distance and lit up a cigarette.

There was a coffee shop across the street. Robert made his way there, politely refusing the solicitations of the female entrepreneurs who propositioned him along the way. He sat down and ordered a cappuccino.

This should take about the right time. An espresso would be too quick.

By the time Robert had finished his cappuccino and paid his bill, Khalil and his shadow were again on the move, this time back toward the metro station. Probably suspecting a tail, Khalil made the same move he had earlier, sending his stalker on a train in the wrong direction. Robert stepped into the last car on Khalil's train, heading in the direction of St. Denis.

Khalil exited the train in the Paris suburb of St. Denis, not only famous for its impressive catholic basilica, but also known for its predominantly Muslim population. As Robert suspected, a man who had been standing outside the station reading a newspaper, rolled it up and began to walk after Khalil had passed him.

Another tail.

Robert stalked the follower, who tailed Khalil to a local Islamic cultural center. Looking around for a good vantage point where he could blend in, Robert found a café on the corner and took a seat. He ordered lunch and settled in for the long haul as his fellow stalker moseyed into a *salon de the* next door.

***

After a week of following Khalil, Robert was getting bored, but the preparations that had to be done were finally finished and he could now begin to formulate a plan. He would use his Ruger .22 with silencer as his principal weapon, with his Glock 17, also with noise suppression, as backup. The Ruger was smaller, not as conspicuous, and would make less of a mess than the Glock. It was an assassin's right hand.

Robert used the lunch hour, which in France was more like three hours, to his advantage. Lunch was almost an inalienable human right in France. The stores were all closed and would be for the next three hours, while the entire city of Paris seemed to shut down, except for the restaurants and cafés, which were filling up with hordes of lunch-goers and would remain full from

12:30 through 3:00 p.m. After the lunch exodus, when everyone went back to work, you would be lucky to get anything but a cup of coffee.

Robert took advantage of the empty streets to slip into Khalil's apartment building unnoticed. Wearing a French postman's uniform and hat, he pushed all the doorbells at the front door of Khalil's building, and declared, *"La Poste! J'ai une livraison pour vous!"* claiming to have a delivery, and shoved the door open when one of the angry residents who had their precious lunch interrupted, buzzed it. He ducked downstairs into the storage cave area and changed into a blonde wig with beret and a light green windbreaker. He checked his watch. According to his established pattern, Khalil should be home within half an hour. Robert went up the stairs to Khalil's floor. The elevator probably had a camera and could be easily monitored. He scanned the corridor of Khalil's apartment for surveillance devices and found none. He had finally "green-lighted" his own mission.

He sequestered himself in an enclave on the side of the elevator and waited. Khalil showed up with the precision of a German train. Robert heard the doors of the lift open and immediately recognized him when he walked out. He waited a beat, followed after him with the Ruger in his hand and called out.

"Excusez-moi, Monsieur?"

Khalil turned. *"Oui?"*

With lightning speed, Robert aimed and fired two shots directly into Khalil's forehead, spattering blood and grey matter against the wall. Khalil collapsed on his back on the floor, his eyes frozen open in a permanent state of surprise.

Robert tucked the windbreaker and wig into his bag, switched it for a non-descript baseball hat, and dropped the gun, which was clean, into a trash receptacle in the lobby. He slipped off his latex gloves, exited the building and calmly walked along with the flow of sidewalk pedestrian traffic right past the plainclothes detective who had been assigned to cover Khalil without even being noticed.

He continued several blocks to the Concorde metro station and rode it to the Franklin Roosevelt stop, where he transferred to line 9 and exited at Ranelagh. It was about a twenty-minute walk home from there. All the excitement had rebuilt Robert's appetite, but there was nothing at home, which meant he would have to wait until at least 8 o'clock before he could get anything decent to eat.

The dog was barking upon Robert's approach to his door and even louder when he inserted his key. When he opened it, he was almost knocked over by a wave of love.

CHAPTER FIFTEEN

After the howling and wrestling of the canine greeting ceremony, Robert fed the dog its dinner and fired up his laptop to check his messages. He didn't have regular email like everyone else. He couldn't afford that digital fingerprint that the NSA, the CIA, the FBI and all the other espionage alphabeticals counted on for their privacy-bashing surveillance of the entire formerly free world. Robert's electronic communications were by encrypted PGP mail in the Internet underworld known as the Darknet. The dog trotted up to Robert, wagging his tail, looked up at him and burped.

"I see you enjoyed your meal." The dog's tongue hung out and he panted. After delving into the Darknet, Robert found an encrypted message that had been sent to his PGP key. Using the key, he decrypted the message:

Bob, this Alexei (Lyosha). I come to Paris next week and it would be great to see you. Please let me know. Cheers.

Seeing the message from Lyosha made his thoughts drift to Lana. He closed his eyes and could smell fresh soap and lavender, see her brilliant blue eyes and feel her soft hair. He thought about calling her for a moment, and then shook his head and put that thought out of his mind.

No connections.

Robert wrote back to Lyosha, using his PGP key:

Of course. I'm waiting for you here in Paris. Call this phone number when you get into town: +33693784642.

Before Robert logged off he heard a snorting sound and looked to his left and down. The big dummy was wagging his long scraggly tail.

"What, buddy? You want to go for a walk or something?"

The dog yelped and jumped in place, his big body flopping around, signifying the affirmative.

"Well, let's go then!"

Robert stood up and headed for the door and the dog made a run for it also, but then sat quietly in the foyer and waited for Robert to open it. He didn't move a muscle until he was given the okay. Robert walked out the door and stood to the side.

"Okay, buddy, you can come out."

The dog ran out the door and immediately sat outside in the corridor, waiting for Robert to lock up.

***

Nathan Anderson scanned the report from the CIA. Adnan Khalil, the target, had been eliminated. So far, his Paladine program was turning out a complete success. Neither he nor Ted Barnard saw terrorism in France as strictly a French threat. France was a melting pot cesspool for thousands of Islamic fanatics who were radicalizing new recruits and sending them out on suicide missions against American, as well as European targets. The roots of terrorism there had to be considered a threat to American interests and must be nipped in the bud at their source, because ultra-liberal, socialist France was not doing anything about it. They were tracking thousands of terrorist suspects, most of them also on the American TSDB (terrorist suspect database), but their enforcement was lacking and their laws and court system archaic. He smiled to himself as he sipped on a cup of steaming black coffee and then set it down to pick up the phone to dial the president.

***

When Robert came back from his walk with the dog, he had already received his next assignment by PGP mail. He studied the secret dossier, memorizing the details. Fahd Naifeh was on both the French and American watch lists. He was wanted in the United States for espionage and terrorism, but the French had refused extradition on the grounds that he was a French citizen. Since the legal system could not capture him, the government had to resort to other methods.

Naifeh was an Iraqi-born financial and banking expert from Turkey who had sided with ISIS during the civil war that had divided the Shiites and Sunnis after the American intervention in Iraq. He was suspected to be a major money launderer for the terrorist group in Europe, but the French government could not amass enough admissible evidence to bring a case against him in their courts. Robert's assignment was to cut through all that red tape and eliminate him from the face of the earth. He studied Naifeh's face and memorized it and his vital statistics. Since France had given up on him, he was less likely to be under surveillance and may be a little easier to take out than Khalil.

***

Naifeh lived in a free-standing townhome in the Ranelagh neighborhood which was dangerously close to Robert's own. It was so close – only two metro stops – he could actually walk to it. When he left his apartment, he was tempted to take the dog, but that would be an identifying factor he could ill afford. Instead, he rode the metro to the Ranelagh station and walked the short two blocks to the residence.

It was the Parisian equivalent of a mansion, a free-standing building of three stories and a basement in a city where most people lived in apartments. Its easy walking distance to the Bois de Boulogne made it a potential site for the assassination, but it depended on Naifeh's habits. Robert needed a place to stake out Naifeh's house and the only candidate was a car on the street, so he went car shopping. He couldn't rent one. That would involve giving his passport and resident card and personal information that could be verified. No – this car would have to be stolen.

CHAPTER SIXTEEN

Robert shopped for his car at the most logical place he could think of – the long-term parking lot at Orly Airport. When he got off the train, he immersed himself in choices at the "car lot" – the parking structure – looking for an automobile with a nice coat of dust on it, as opposed to a squeaky clean one or one with a thick coat. That signified one that, most likely, had been left a while and should sit there a little longer. He found one candidate, a Peugeot 308.

Doesn't fit the neighborhood. Not fancy enough.

He kept looking, going from floor to floor and row to row. Finally, he found his prize – a white Range Rover Sport. He popped open the car door with a slim jim and the alarm immediately went off. As it wailed, he calmly and quickly plugged in a handy Chinese reprogramming device he had purchased on-line and reprogrammed an extra generic key fob in two minutes flat. The only glitch was presenting himself at the exit. He paid for the parking plus an extra fine for losing his entrance ticket.

Robert stopped at a gas station and ran the car through the automated car wash to make it presentable for the neighborhood, then drove "home" in the new Range Rover. He circled around the street several times until he found the best parking space he could; one that gave him an adequate view of the front of Naifeh's mansion. From that point on it was a waiting game.

The hours droned on and Naifeh remained indoors. In the tedium of the stakeout, Robert's thoughts ran rampant, imagining the soft, warm, exciting presence of Lana mixed with feelings of contempt for Gregory Manizek. He snacked on a baguette and cheese while he waited. There was nothing much going on in the street. A few were passers-by, likely headed for the forest, but most people were probably at work.

Finally, late in the afternoon, Naifeh exited his villa alone and began walking toward the Ranelagh metro station.

Even rich people ride the metro. Good way to beat traffic.

Robert donned his knit beret and got out of the Rover. He followed Naifeh to the metro station, lingering back so he could observe if he was the only one doing so. Naifeh proved to be less evasive than Khalil had, patiently waiting on the platform for his train, and not making any last-minute switches. He boarded the train along with all of the other passengers and Robert stayed one car back.

With Robert silently in tow, Naifeh exited at the Opera Station, making his way up the stairs into the famous plaza, and its centerpiece, the Opéra Garnier, which was surrounded on almost all sides by private banking branches of the well-known and unknown banks of the world. He steered himself into the Bank of Turkey, and disappeared behind its revolving door.

Bank of Turkey – makes sense.

Robert knew ISIS financed its operations and managed its money by dummy companies trading through money exchanges in Istanbul, which operated on a "trust" basis, with extremely high commissions. It was only logical some of that money would find its way into Turkish banks.

No wonder they want him taken out. It must be almost impossible to stop them from connecting with the international banking world.

Naifeh remained inside the bank for about forty minutes, and then was on the move again. He headed across the street toward Galeries Lafayette. Robert followed Naifeh through the front entrance and into the grand domed superstore with its gilded arches. The main part of the building was round, like the Capitol building, with three upper floors opening onto the main floor below, like balconies in the opera house across the street. Above the top floor, the huge illuminated ceiling of the rotunda looked like the inside of a kaleidoscope perched on top of a row of church-like stained glass windows. The opulent Parisian department store was exactly as it appeared: The ultimate symbol of western world decadence.

Hmm. Another devout Muslim.

Naifeh navigated through the first floor's perfume, cosmetic and jewelry counters, stopping at Rolex to admire the watches. The salesgirl held out a 20,000-euro watch for him to examine, and, as he handled it, Robert couldn't help but be reminded of the way he had seen his dog drool for a steak bone.

Surprised he's not drooling. He must have made a good deal at the bank.

Naifeh tried on a watch and held it up to the light in an almost feminine way. Robert was getting quite enough of him.

Can't wait to waste this guy.

Naifeh purchased the watch with cash. After he had made this investment with the money gleaned from the blood of countless refugees, he headed up the escalator and Robert followed him to the second floor, where he made his way across the connecting bridge to the men's store. Robert followed him to the shoe department, where he observed another tedious process of trying on the most expensive shoes in the world. The shoe department had many different boutiques, representing the various marks of fine shoes. Robert took a seat in front of a rack of Prada footwear and watched Naifeh.

"Puis vous j'aider?"

Robert turned his attention from Naifeh to a middle-aged saleswoman, offering her help.

"Non, merci. J'attends quel qu'un."

Naifeh's own salesperson was building a virtual tower with shoe boxes. Finally, the terrorist banker settled on a pair of brown Berlutis for 1800 euros.

After he had spent more money in the store than most of his compatriots make in ten years, Naifeh exited with his shopping bags and grabbed a taxi at the taxi stand. Robert did the same, hoping not to lose him. The driver was an Arab who could have passed for Naifeh's brother. Robert instructed the driver to pursue the escaping cab.

"Suivez lui."

"De quoi vous parlez?"

Robert shoved a 100 euro bill under his nose and he got the idea.

"Le taxi la! Allez!"

The driver took off down the grand boulevard, using its width to navigate a place behind Naifeh's taxi. The taxi pulled to a stop in the 5th Arrondissement at the Grand Mosque of Paris and Naifeh disappeared through the archway under a golden half-moon and star symbol.

Ah, he's going to thank Allah for all his little gifts. Don't worry, scumbag, I'll make sure you can thank him in person. And soon.

CHAPTER SEVENTEEN

Naifeh taxied home with his conscience clear and with his new purchases and settled in for the night. Robert watched with field glasses as he trudged up the steps to his front door, and then bent over and felt under the flowerpot and withdrew a key. He opened the door without disarming an alarm and placed the key back under the pot. It was too good to be true.

He spent the next few days and nights watching Naifeh and concluded he was not being tailed, which was a good thing. The French had given up on him. But the boredom of sitting in the car for hours on end and following the hypocritical Muslim around Paris was becoming too much for Robert to bear. His only breaks were to walk home the back way, through the forest, to let the dog out twice a day. Tedium was not the only issue. He didn't know when the owner of the Rover was coming back, but once he did, he was sure to report the car stolen. It had to be returned as soon as possible. It had become, out of necessity, Naifeh's time to die.

Robert sketched out a homicidal plan in his mind, covering every possible detail and contingency. With even the best plans, there was always at least a 20% margin of error because of unknown variables. Robert went over the plan again and again in his head, trying to cut the margin down. When he was satisfied, he headed for the airport to drop off the car. He stopped at the *Total* filling station and filled the tank to the approximate amount it had been when he had picked it up. He parked in the vacuum stall and vacuumed the car thoroughly, wiped it clean, and headed for the airport. He parked it in the same lot, in almost the same place as the exact one it had been parked in when he had taken it. He took the parking ticket with him and put the car out of his memory as he walked away from it, discarding the ripped-up ticket in the metro station.

When Robert arrived home, he checked his PGP mail before taking the dog for its evening walk. Lyosha was due to arrive the following week. This meant the job had to be done by Sunday. Robert arranged his tools: A Sig Sauer P226 Mosquito with noise suppressor, his backup Glock 9mm with silencer, black jeans, black sweatshirt and black ski mask. If Naifeh was true to his patterns, he would be home every day by 9 p.m. and in bed by midnight.

***

The following day, Robert spot-checked Naifeh's place to confirm he was home by the usual time. He went back home and took the dog with him to his favorite Italian restaurant in the neighborhood. The dog sat dutifully under the table. He knew whatever was left over would be his, so begging was unnecessary. Robert ordered a *quatre fromage* pizza for an appetizer, followed by a bloody steak with a generous bone that could also be claimed by the dog if he behaved. After the meal, he threw the "pizza bones" one-at-a time to the dog, which skillfully caught each one and swallowed them without chewing. He saved the piece de résistance for last, bagging it up for home. The dog walked along Robert's side, sticking his big snout in the air to sniff the aromas from the bag. When they got home, Robert unwrapped the bone and put it on the floor while the dog patiently waited, with 100% of his attention focused on the mass of osseous matter until Robert gave the go-ahead, then he charged at it, took it in his mouth, and went to the corner to chew on it.

Later that night (morning really), while Butthead was still chomping feverishly on his bone, Robert suited up, holstered up, and left the apartment. He proceeded to Ranelagh on foot, through the forest and approached it from outside the city limits. At the corner, from the cover of a clump of trees and in the shadows, he used his field glasses to check the house. Nobody was on the street and the lights were off in Naifeh's bedroom. His time was up.

He quietly approached the house, donned his gloves, and lifted the flowerpot. Taking the key, he unlocked the door, and opened it silently, then replaced the key where he had found it. He slipped on his surgeon's booties and a surgical cap and went inside.

There were sounds coming from the back of the house. Robert could see one of the posterior rooms was illuminated with light. Naifeh was still up. He ducked into a side room. It appeared to be a sitting room of sorts. The house was as lavishly furnished as Naifeh's sanctimonious lifestyle, filled with antique Louis XIV and XV furniture with delicate golden legs and Venetian crystal chandeliers. It looked like a museum or one of the apartments in Versailles. In the twisted version of ISIS Islam, being rich was *haram*. This meant Naifeh was a sinner, and Robert would only be so happy to deliver him a one-way ticket straight to hell.

The doorbell rang.

Shit! He has a visitor! Maybe they'll go away.

Naifeh passed right by Robert to answer the door. He heard small talk coming from the foyer and then the clacking of a woman's high-heeled shoes on the marble floor. As the sounds came closer, Robert realized they were heading straight for this room. He crouched behind a large Louis XIV purple velour couch and hoped they wouldn't see him. Otherwise, things would be a lot sloppier than he had planned.

Hopefully there won't be any more guests.

Naifeh invited the woman into the sitting room. Robert could see her slender bare legs and ultra-high red pumps. The room began to fill with the smell of a French perfume boutique, where it was not uncommon to take a "shower" in perfume to try it on. He seated her precisely on the couch Robert was hiding behind.

She's obviously a hooker. More haram.

Naifeh withdrew and came back with a bottle of champagne and two glasses. He popped the cork and it flew over the couch, almost hitting Robert in the head. Both of them laughed at the flight of the champagne cork.

Naifeh began to make small talk with the girl as they drank. Robert was feeling cramped behind the couch and had a right mind to deny Naifeh his last orgasm and send both of them on their way out, but he hung in there. When the conversation died away, Robert heard only the sound of her breathing heavily, mixed with masculine guttural grunts and groans. They were making out, which was making Robert disgusted.

Finally, they stood up and walked out of the room and Robert could hear the stairs creaking as they walked up to the bedroom. Robert took a more comfortable seat in the sitting room and waited. After about forty minutes, Naifeh and the girl emerged at the bottom of the stairs and Robert heard her clacking her way out amid the sound of mutual good-byes. Naifeh went back upstairs.

After about an hour, Robert quietly padded up the stairs to the first floor, turned right and paused outside Naifeh's room. He could hear Naifeh snoring in post-coital bliss. Robert entered the opulent bedroom, which was completely dark. He unsheathed the Sig, walked up to Naifeh, who was calmly sleeping on his Egyptian cotton satin sheets, and cupped his hand over his mouth while he pushed his head against the goose down pillow with the gun. Naifeh's eyes opened in terror. Robert calmly addressed him in his perfect Arabic.

"No this is not a dream, Naifeh. *Allah la yardaa.* I'm here to make sure you get to Jahannam."

Beads of sweat popped out on Naifeh's forehead. He shivered, tried to speak. Robert fired into the terrorist's forehead. Then he looked around the room. Naifeh's new Rolex was on the nightstand. He took it and a wad of cash from his wallet, also on the nightstand, to make it look like a robbery.

Robert cracked the glass panel in the kitchen door that lead to the backyard and opened it. He slipped out the front and faded away. He dipped into the forest and walked to the edge of the pond, where he chucked the Rolex and the gun. He would anonymously donate the cash to a mosque the next day.

CHAPTER EIGHTEEN

Lyosha's arrival in Paris was like a moving party. Robert went to the airport ahead of time to meet him and rented a car for their escapades. Standing in the arrivals area, he could see Lyosha's smiling face towering above the bobbing heads of the crowd. The smile remained as he greeted Robert with his "death grip" handshake.

"So happy to see you, my American friend. Just like Gene Kelly."

Robert's eyebrows raised in surprise. "Gene Kelly?"

"An American in Paris. This is Paris, right?"

"Yeah, so?"

"So, you are the American. An American in Paris, just like Gene Kelly."

"Don't expect me to dance around for you."

Lyosha's rolling laughter almost knocked Robert off his feet. Robert knew Lyosha expected him to show him Paris like Lyosha had shown him Moscow, so they set off immediately for the center of the city. But strolling around the city was not Lyosha's idea of a visit to Paris. After visiting some of Robert's favorite landmarks, Lyosha asked the ten thousand dollar question.

"What about *kuritsa*? Chicks?"

"Tonight. There will be chicks tonight."

Robert treated him to an ample meal at *Brasserie Bofinger* in the heart of the Bastille – mounds of oysters, clams, shrimp, langoustine, lobster and crab heaped on a huge bowl of ice. They inhaled the oysters, between helpings of freshly baked bread smothered in fine butter, and then attacked the remaining sea jewels. By the time they were finished, two waiters stood before them with the freshly grilled carcasses of two large sea bass.

"There is more? After all that?"

Robert smiled. Now it was his turn to spoil Lyosha. As they feasted, the wine flowed freely and it wasn't long before they had polished off two bottles between themselves.

After dinner, they stepped outside to walk off their huge dinner in preparation for the night's festivities. The night was filled with revelers leaving restaurants and the modern opera house, and hordes of students hanging out in and in front of the bars surrounding the Place de Bastille, only a few paces away. Lyosha looked at the base of the monument, which had been defaced, with curiosity.

"Why they allow this for their monuments? It's covered with all this graffiti and shit."

Lyosha pointed to the tagging all over the base of the monument, a Corinthian column topped by Dumont's *"Génie de la Liberté"* that towered over the square to mark the site of the Bastille prison, stormed by French revolutionaries on July 14, 1789. The scrawling contained phrases like "Je suis Charlie" and "Fuck terrorism."

"This "graffiti" and shit is all in memory of the Charlie Hebdo massacres."

Lyosha's expression of disgust turned to anger. "Fucking terrorists. I would like to kill every one of them."

Robert nodded. It was a desire they had in common.

***

Robert parked the car in an underground parking in the George V neighborhood near the Champs Élysées. It was close to Lyosha's hotel and, if their evening tonight was anything like the ones they had in Moscow, nobody was going to be in any shape to drive home. They took a table at the legendary Crazy Horse Café and watched the girls dancing in a nude can-can show as they polished off an ice-cold bottle of Titomirov vodka in an illuminated ice bucket.

"You ordered Titomirov!"

"Of course. I remembered how much you like it. Nothing but the best for you!"

Lyosha raised his glass to Robert and looked into his eyes.

"To my American friend. May we always be on the same side, fighting those asshole terrorists together."

Robert clicked his full shot glass.

"*Do adna!* To the end!" Lyosha declared, meaning Robert had to drink the glass in one gulp to the end. Robert nodded and they both simultaneously slammed down the icy hot liquid.

After one bottle had been polished off, they retired to the VIP room, where they secured another private table, at an additional commitment to buy an even more outrageously expensive bottle of vodka.

"Boab, do you realize that, in Russia, for this price, we would have each already had harem of girls, and not just to look at?"

Robert laughed. Minutes later a cocktail waitress in a mini skirt carried a shiny chrome ice bucket to their table. A sparkler was blazing in the top of the bottle as the waitress set the illuminated monstrosity on their table. After the sparkler had burned out and they had their first drink, tall girls in scanty dresses began parading by them, showing their wares in hopes for a lap dance or two. They were in luck. Lyosha had his eye set on one of his blue-eyed, blonde haired countrywomen. As she bounced on his lap, he spoke with her in Russian and discovered her name was Anastasia (Nastya) and charmed her into coming home with him after work. After a few songs on top of Lyosha, she retreated to the stage for her performance.

"I think I will have a good night."

Robert nodded. "I would say so."

"Boab, do you ever talk to that girl you met in Moscow – Svetlana?"

Robert shook his head. "No."

"Why not? Russian girl like her would love to come to Paris."

Robert shrugged. "I don't know."

"You not like her?"

"I do, I do."

"Then what is problem? We call her now."

Lyosha reached in his jacket pocket for his cell phone.

"No, no, it's much too late."

"Okay, tomorrow then." He slipped the phone back.

"Tomorrow."

After Robert's wallet had taken a huge beating settling the bill, they stood up from the table. Lyosha's arm was locked around Nastya's waist.

"Boab, why you no have girl?"

Robert smiled. "It's okay."

Lyosha shook his head. "No, not okay. We get you girl. He asked Nastya something in Russian. Robert put his hands out, shaking them in a stopping motion. "Really, really, it's not necessary."

"Boab, you are man, right?"

"Yes."

"And you are not gay?"

"No."

"Or married?"

"No."

"Then, my friend, it is absolutely necessary. It is like drinking or breathing. You don't want to die, do you?"

"No."

By then, three of Nastya's Russian friends had lined up in front of them, and they were all smiling at Robert like mice looking at a juicy piece of cheese.

"These girls all go home from work now. Choose."

Avoiding the blondes, Robert chose a brunette with green eyes, so he wouldn't be reminded of Lana.

CHAPTER NINETEEN

Rue du Ranelagh was cluttered with blue and white police cars, their red and blue lights flashing, when Inspector Soussier pulled up to the villa at No. 16 which was the center of all the commotion. He double-parked his car outside, exited and approached the two uniformed policemen at the entrance of the villa.

"What do we have here?"

One of the uniformed cops responded proudly. He had been the first on the scene.

"A man has been murdered in his bed, sir. Looks like a burglary. I have secured the crime scene."

"What's your name?"

"Franco, sir."

Soussier strapped on a pair of booties and popped on some latex gloves. He gave a set to Franco, who stared at them first, then got the idea.

"Put these on and come with me. What makes you think this was a burglary?"

Franco slipped the booties on and struggled to keep up with Soussier, who was on a mission.

"Well, for one thing, sir, there was a glass door broken in the kitchen. I figure that's how he got in."

Inspector Soussier humphed as he mounted the stairs with Franco in tow. "What else?"

"We found a receipt in his wallet for a Rolex he bought last week at Galeries Lafayette, but no watch and his wallet was empty. No cash."

"Maybe he uses only credit cards."

They entered the bedroom and Soussier came up to the bed and leaned in over it to take a good look at the body.

"Anybody touch the body?"

"No, sir. Looks like a single shot to the head."

"Yes, Franco, what this looks like is a professional hit. I'd say a .22 caliber weapon at close range. I don't suppose the neighbors heard anything?"

"No, sir."

"Let's find out if they saw anything unusual at all. Send some of your men door to door. I want names and statements."

"Yes, sir."

"What is this poor fellow's name, Franco?"

"It's Naifeh, Fahd Naifeh. A Turkish banker."

Soussier's eyebrows puckered. "Do you know who this is, Franco?"

"Yes, sir. I just told you."

"I mean, this is the guy they tried to prosecute for being the main banker for the Islamic State. He was just acquitted on money laundering and terrorism financing charges."

Franco perked up. "I didn't know that, sir."

Soussier scratched his head. "This is very similar to another case I'm working on – also an ISIS suspect by the name of Khalil. You heard of him?"

"No, sir."

***

Robert woke up to a headache and the sound of the shower. He then remembered he had brought a house guest home last night. Yana came out of the bathroom smelling like fresh soap and perfume and refused Robert's overtures to have breakfast at the bakery down the street.

"Not even a coffee? I can make some here."

"No, I have to get back. Have work tonight."

She pecked him on the cheek and was out the door, leaving the apartment quiet and the dog wagging its tail with curiosity.

Robert didn't expect to hear from Lyosha until the afternoon, so he checked his PGP mail and found another assignment waiting. Mahmud Shamoun was a suspected ISIS terrorist who had immigrated to France about a year ago as a refugee. He had been suspected by the authorities of aiding and abetting terrorist groups, but the French, as usual, claimed they couldn't find sufficient evidence to prosecute him. The evidence Robert was presented was on a video which had matched Shamoun's identity card with the use of facial recognition software. It showed a young Shamoun in a group of terrorists waving machine guns, and then gunning down an American journalist in Syria. That was all the evidence Robert required, and he began planning how to end Shamoun's terroristic career immediately.

***

Inspector Nicolas Soussier ran his fingers over the keyboard, searching on the Internet for information about a closed investigation in the States regarding a vigilante who had been killing terrorists the social media had named "Paladine." Most of the articles he had found referred to an Arizona case investigated by a detective Joshua Maynard. Soussier stayed late in the office so he could phone Maynard about the case.

"Detective Maynard?"

"Yes?"

"This is Inspector Nicolas Soussier from the Police Nationale in Paris. We have a case here that is remarkably similar to your Paladine case, and I wanted to talk to you about it."

Maynard's heart jumped. He had never given up on the Paladine case, but every lead he had found seemed to have gone stale. Maybe he was in France now.

"That case was closed."

"I know, Detective, but I wonder if you may be able to send over your files so we can study them for similarities."

"There are a lot of files."

"Can you send them electronically?"

"Yes, I'd be happy to. Inspector?"

"Yes?"

"If you find something interesting, can you please let me know? This case is of utmost interest to me."

"Of course."

Soussier waited several hours into the night for the information to arrive by download link, and delved into it right away. Maynard had been tenacious in his pursuit of the case, but Soussier gave a new meaning to the word.

CHAPTER TWENTY

Lyosha had checked in with Robert too late in the afternoon to have lunch. Unlike Moscow, where you could get breakfast, lunch or dinner at any hour of the day or night, 24 hours around the clock, since lunch was like a religious service in France, the restaurants stopped serving it at 3 p.m., so Lyosha, on Robert's advice, ordered room service. His only breakfast had been a pot of coffee and another helping of Nastya, so he was famished. Robert made plans to meet him later on for dinner. In the meantime, he formulated a strategy for taking care of Shamoun.

Since Robert had some time, he set out to begin the process of surveilling Shamoun. The jihadist lived in the Bastille area of Paris, a place normally thriving with students, mostly because of the cheap rent. As a result, it also had its share of scumbags. Shamoun lived in a less scummy part of the neighborhood near the river. Robert took his motorcycle there to scope it out. Shamoun's building was on the Quai de la Rapée, almost directly across from the metro station of the same name. His fourth floor apartment had one wall made almost entirely of glass that would have given him a very good vantage of anyone or anything approaching from below. Robert parked his motorcycle past the building, and casually walked by it, snapping pictures surreptitiously with his phone as he pretended to talk on it "hands free." As he passed by, he noticed two guards standing watch in the courtyard below. From that he assumed Shamoun must be ready to move soon. He took a seat in a local café near where he had parked, ordered a coffee, and waited.

After about twenty minutes, Shamoun's entourage was on the move. There were the two bodyguards Robert had seen out front, Shamoun, and then two others – a parade of dark suits with beards. They ushered Shamoun into a black Mercedes parked almost right next to Robert's bike. Robert waited a beat before pursuing them. He supposed the extra security was because they had either been alerted to the previous two ISIS hits, or Shamoun had always taken these precautions. Either way, it was obvious to Robert he was not a lower occupant on the chain of command. Shamoun was important to them.

The Mercedes took off down the quai, which hugged the River Seine and its magnificent bridges, and Robert followed under cover of traffic so he could not be seen. In this area, at any time, there were always a number of motorbikes and scooters, so blending in was easy. After a short scenic drive by the River Seine, they made their way to the cesspool outside of Paris which was St. Denis, home to tenement slums of State supplemented housing, containing over 600,000 Muslims, and parked not too far from a local mosque. The five, conspicuously devoid of any police surveillance, proceeded to a corner coffee shop, where they hung out for over an hour.

What is he up to in there?

With Shamoun's background, it couldn't be anything good.

***

When Robert arrived home, a stranger was waiting in front of his building. Average height, very cop-looking. Robert activated the door and began to push it in.

"Mr. Garcia?"

"Yes?"

"I'm Inspector Soussier from the French police. May I have a word with you?"

"Sure, come on in."

Robert held the door open for the Inspector and showed him in. He rode with him in the elevator to the second floor and led him to the apartment. When they approached the door, the dog was barking loudly.

"You have a dog."

"Don't worry. Just don't make any sudden moves and everything will be fine."

The Inspector stood there nervously as Robert opened the door. The dog's nose poked through as he pushed it open. It was growling.

"It's okay, Butthead. Stand down."

The dog obeyed, but kept a watchful eye on Soussier as he stepped inside and Robert closed the door behind him.

"Don't worry. Come in, have a seat."

Soussier sat down in one of the Ikea arm chairs in the living room and the dog sat in front of him, staring at him.

"Is he always like this?"

"Only with strangers. He'll be fine."

"Why did you name him *Butthead*?"

"Look at him. He's butt ugly. You can't tell the face from the rear end."

Soussier turned his head to look at the dog, which curled its lip. All he could seem to see was teeth, and rear ends usually weren't equipped with those.

"How can I help you, Inspector?"

"I'm working on a homicide case and your name came up in association with it."

"My name?" Robert looked at him, curiously.

"Yes. I've been reviewing the files of a Detective Maynard from Arizona. You were identified as one of the suspects in a case he was working on."

"I was cleared in that case, Inspector. They were profiling veterans who had been in Special Forces. I fit the profile. There are a lot of us who do."

The Inspector nodded and flashed a phony French smile with impudence.

"Just the same, it's quite a coincidence, isn't it, that you would be in Paris at the same time as a series of jihadist murders?"

"Jihadist murders?"

"You haven't heard?"

"I try not to pay attention to the news. Too depressing."

"Of course." The Inspector brushed off his sleeve and looked again in the direction of the dog, which was following his every move. "I am investigating the murder of a suspected ISIS recruiter as well as a suspected terrorist banker."

"So you want to find whoever did it so you can give them a medal or what?"

Another grin. "Very funny, Mr. Garcia. No matter what their alleged terrorist affiliations, these were murders and murder is against the law."

"Of course. But you have to pardon me because I can't imagine how I could possibly help you."

"Can you tell me where you were Wednesday night, from about midnight to 4 a.m.?"

"I was home."

"Do you have any witnesses?"

Robert motioned to the dog with his head. "Just Butthead here. He's my only roommate."

Soussier looked at the dog. The direct eye contact provoked another baring of its teeth.

"I see. Well, if I have any more questions, can I feel free to call on you?"

"Of course. Anytime."

Soussier stood up from his chair and the dog jumped to attention, on alert.

"It's okay, really."

Robert walked the Inspector to the door. Besides the corps de guard on Shamoun, he also had a cop up his ass. The next job was not going to be easy.

***

Robert was not very good at having friends, but Lyosha made it easy. He took him to an Asian restaurant off the Champs Élysées with excellent cuisine. Instead of vodka, Lyosha settled for sake.

"This Asian vodka is not so strong, is it Boab?"

Robert sipped at his sake which brought on a strange face from Lyosha.

"Boab, no sipping. Drink like a man." Lyosha downed another small terra cotta cup of sake in one gulp like it was a shot of vodka.

"This is sake, Lyosha. It's kind of like wine."

Lysoha started at him. "*Do adna*!" He laughed.

Robert slammed the sake. It was warm and soothing. He had discovered a new way to drink it.

They spent the rest of the evening poking around the stores on the Champs Élysées until the night clubs opened, for another long night of drinking and carousing. This was Lyosha's idea of the perfect vacation. Despite Lyosha's insistence, Robert did not bring a girl home this time, and he limited himself on the alcohol. He had to be alert at all times now that he was under the watchful eyes of the French police.

CHAPTER TWENTY-ONE

Inspector Soussier's meeting with the coroner went as he thought it would. The cause of death was a single shot to the head with a small caliber bullet, probably a .22. There was evidence Naifeh had ejaculated shortly before death, and long, bleached hairs had been found on his bedsheets. That meant a woman was either the murderer or it was the obvious. In any event, she had to be located because she was one of the last persons to ever see him alive. The DNA testing would take a while, so he concentrated on the reports of the other physical evidence on the scene. There was a rap on his glass door and he looked up to see Franco, smiling

"Come in, officer."

"Inspector, I want to thank you for allowing me to work this case with you."

"No need to thank me, Franco. You were the first on the scene. To the first go the spoils, usually. What have you got?"

Franco spread a few sheets of paper on Soussier's desk.

"We got a positive identification on one of the latent fingerprints, sir. The woman has a rap sheet for prostitution."

Soussier looked at the report. "Why am I not surprised?"

"Do you want me to bring her in, Inspector?"

"Yes, please. I'd like to talk to her."

"Is she a suspect?"

"Well, we can't rule anything out, Franco, but I doubt it."

Franco's look was that of disappointment.

"Police work isn't usually that easy."

***

When Robert finally dropped Lyosha off at the airport, he made a mental note to himself to visit him in Moscow. This trip had been complicated by work and the worry of a new element of danger from Inspector Soussier. Robert's first trip to Russia had been cut off by the same type of interruptions and he promised himself he would return someday to set it right. After dropping Lyosha off, he turned in the rental car and took the train home, plotting out his next moves in his head, like a chess game against an unknown and mysterious opponent.

Walking home from the metro station, he could see a pair of plainclothes officers parked in a green Renault just a few paces from his apartment. He doubled back, crossed the street to the *boulangerie* and bought a baguette, then went next door to the *fromagerie* and selected some cheese, and finally to the wine store, the third shop in the neighborhood trilogy, where he selected a red wine to pair with it. On the way back home, he stopped at the Renault and tapped on the window. The cop in the passenger's side rolled it down.

"Oui?"

"Pour vous." Robert held out his hands with the culinary gifts. The surprised sleuth instinctively latched on to them and Robert let go and walked on.

"Mai, attendez! Attendez!"

The man called out and exited the car, holding the packages and Robert waved back to him.

"Bon apetitt!"

Robert waved with the back of his hand as he walked on. When he arrived home, he snubbed the dog, which kept jumping around and whining to signify his arrival.

"Shut up, Butthead!"

The watching eyes outside made Robert uneasy. Being under surveillance added an extra component of danger to an already dangerous occupation. He removed his electronic bug detection equipment from the closet and began to sweep the room.

"Has anybody been in here, boy?"

After ten minutes, he had assured himself it was clean, but Robert's paranoid mentality would not let it rest. He revised his practice to hack into wireless Internet connections at cafés in the future. If they were monitoring his Internet connection, they could not decrypt his messages, but they would sure be able to tell he was sending them out encrypted.

He grabbed his laptop and headed for the door, only to find it blocked by the big dumb dog.

"Get out of the way, dumbass!"

He whimpered and hung his head low.
"All right, all right, come on."

The dog happily wagged its tail as Robert opened the door and the dog flew out of it. He walked briskly to the corner and crossed the street, doubled back and continued, all the while looking for a tail. Halfway to Butthead's favorite walking park they stopped at Robert's favorite

French restaurant. Taking an inside seat next to the window, Robert ordered escargots for an appetizer, followed by filet mignon. He opened his laptop, hacking into the WiFi from the design shop next door which was closed for lunch. His fingers flew over the keys, composing a message to the anonymous head of covert operations, Gregory Manizek:

Heat is on. I cannot fulfill this task. Request reassignment immediately.

He slapped the top down on the computer.

"*Tout va bien*, Monsieur Robert?"

Robert looked up at an inquisitive waiter, who was holding a bottle of red wine, showing him the label.

"*Oh, oui, oui.*"

The waiter poured a small splash of wine for him to taste, and Robert put the glass to his lips and swilled.

"*C'est bon.*"

The glass was filled with St. Émilon and the bottle set on the table. Robert picked up the glass and peered through the rich red liquid. He took a sip and put it down. By that time, the escargot had already arrived and the dog was standing at attention, wagging his tail. Robert turned his head to him.

"You think you're getting some now?"

The dog hung its head.

"That's right. You have to wait."

The dog collapsed in a heap on the floor by the table as Robert ate the escargot. He only perked up when the waiter put the filet on the table. By the end of the meal, Robert switched his computer back on and found a reply to his message:

Negative. Continue the course.

Robert angrily typed back: *Need to speak with you, in person.*

For a free agent, Robert was beginning to feel a lot like an employee. Or a slave.

***

Robert knew there was no way he was getting out of this latest assignment. It would have to be done. What he would do after this was undecided. He continued with his preparations despite the complications on both sides.

Day by day, he left his apartment with a police tail on his ass. They had not yet found where Robert garaged his motorcycle and, if they did, it was game over. At that point, he wouldn't be able to move it. So, he played a constant game of hide-and-seek with the cops, which slowed the entire process down. Leaving his apartment, Robert used standard countersurveillance to escape the tail, and then descended into a metro station two blocks away to catch the number 10 line to connect to the number 9, instead of using the station right on his own street. From there, he exited another two stations away from the garage and walked the rest of the way. Eventually, they would beef up their surveillance efforts, so Robert changed his patterns frequently.

When he finally reached the garage, he took off on the motorcycle toward Quai de la Rapée, to do his own surveillance on Mahmud Shamoun. There appeared to be no break in Shamoun's security force. They guarded him wherever he went, and he was never in the open. His suited goons surrounded him at all times, providing the perfect cocoon for his ingress and egress in every open space.

As usual, Shamoun headed for the Paris suburb of St. Denis, and, per his habitude, he and his group frequented a local coffee shop near the run-down public housing units known in France as "HLM" (*Habitation à Loyer Modéré*). Robert was starting to notice a pattern of hordes of Arab youths flocking to the coffee shops whenever Shamoun was there.

Is he a recruiter or what? I have to find out what's going on in there.

To observe, he had to be where Shamoun would be before he got there, so as not to cause notice to himself. Based on Shamoun's patterns, the odds were about 1-in-4 that he would be sitting in the correct coffee shop at the right time. Robert rented a small dive in the area so as not to be a stranger in their midst. He used the little apartment as a home base, going home only at night. That way, he could let the dog out at night and again early the next morning, leaving the bulk of the day to concentrate on his subject.

Robert stashed his motorcycle at a parking near Place de Clichy and rode the metro to a different station in St. Denis every day. His dark skin and hair, along with his prowess in the language of Arabia made blending in not an onerous task. Robert was a dead-ringer for one of "them," which meant he could run in their circles with a minimum of suspicion. Being a dead ringer, however, didn't prevent the risk of ending up really dead himself.

CHAPTER TWENTY-TWO

Robert awoke to barking and buzzing at the visitor-friendly hour of 5:30 a.m. He swung his legs out of bed and his bare feet hit the cold tile floor. He rubbed his eyes and looked at the clock.

Shit.

"J'arrive, j'arrive!"

He shuffled to the door, scratched his butt and looked through the peephole.

Cops.

Robert unbolted the door. Standing in front of him, cup of coffee in his hand, was Inspector Soussier.

It's Lieutenant Columbo.

"Good morning, Mr. Garcia."

"Morning? It's still dark outside."

"I've been trying to talk to you. Trouble is I can never catch you at home. May I come in?"

Robert stood aside, making a sweeping motion with his hand. The intruder entered, spouting his French faux politesse as Robert shut the door.

"Thank you. May I have a seat?"

"Be my guest."

Soussier put one foot into the apartment and received a friendly greeting of a dog's nose in his crotch, growling.

"Don't worry about him. Just don't make any fast moves. Down, boy!"

The dog stood down and Soussier perched himself on one of the armchairs and set his coffee cup on the table. Robert and the dog remained standing.

"We've been missing each other lately."

"You could have called, Inspector."

"What keeps you so busy these days?"

"My private business, I suppose."

Soussier humphed and cleared his throat.

"So what did you want to talk to me about?"

"I'm a little puzzled about this case I'm working on."

"That's what detectives do, isn't it? Work on puzzles?"

Soussier smiled slyly, and continued. "I thought maybe you could help me."

"I really don't have any experience in police work. I'm afraid I wouldn't make a very good consultant."

Soussier pretended not to hear the response as he opened his briefcase and spread some pictures out on the table next to his coffee cup.

"Recognize any of them?"

Robert looked casually at the photographs of the dead Adnan Khalil and Fahd Naifeh and shook his head. "Should I?"

"Look closely."

Robert looked again, devoid of emotion or interest. He shrugged his shoulders. Soussier peered at him, intently.

"What's the first thing that comes to mind?"

"I don't know. That these guys must have a hell of a migraine?"

"Very funny. You can see why I think these were both professional hits, and both by the same killer."

"Not really. I'm not the cop, you are."

Soussier ignored the comment and kept barreling. "Both were shot at close range and both with a .22 caliber weapon, we figure with sound suppressor."

Robert acted like it was the first time he had heard the terms. "We can feel safer with you on the job, Inspector."

"So then, nothing?"

Robert shook his head.

"Then you wouldn't mind if I took a look around?"

"Where, here?"

Robert held his hands palms up, questioning him. "Am I a suspect?"

"Let's just say you're a person of interest, but you knew that, didn't you?"

"I can't imagine why."

"So I can take a look?"

"Sure, just show me your warrant and you can have at it."

Soussier frowned. "You know I don't have one."

Robert shrugged and the Inspector scooped up his photographs, slipped them back in the case and zipped it up. He stood and faced Robert.

"Next time, call so you can be sure to catch me at home."

Soussier grinned slyly. "Oh, we *will* catch you, Mr. Garcia. Don't worry."

CHAPTER TWENTY-THREE

Robert sped up his readiness process, aware there were probably extra men placed on his surveillance and he would have to be not only vigilant, but clever to avoid them. He poured a couple cups of coffee and took them and the dog outside. When they stopped at the unmarked police vehicle, Butthead hiked his leg and peed on the front wheel as Robert knocked on the window with his elbow. One of the cops rolled it down.

"Oui?"

"Coffee, for you." Robert held the Styrofoam cups out to the officer. "It's going to be a long day."

The cop took the cups from his outstretched hand, instinctively, and, also out of instinct, said *"Merci."*

"Mai, je vous en prie." Robert saluted to the cops and he and the dog took off in a jog down the street toward the forest. The policeman put the cups on the dashboard and followed Robert with his eyes until he turned the corner. Then he stumbled out of the car and picked up his pace to keep in sight of his subject.

Robert and the dog crossed the multi-street intersection and broke into a brisk run toward the forest, disappearing into a trail hidden by a clump of trees. The cop reached the intersection and his head spun around, as if he was confused. Making a decision, he trotted across the street.

Robert finally ended his walk, making sure he had not been seen, at the home of his dog sitter, who was only too happy to take the dog in on no notice. He thanked her and then slipped down the street to the nearest metro station and down into it. He rode the metro to his garage, picked up his bike, and, given the hour, headed straight for St. Denis without stopping.

***

Mahmud Shamoun and his men were already seated in a corner of the third café Robert visited. He walked in and took a seat. From his peripherals, he could see they had a larger crowd than usual. A couple of his goons looked pretty nervous.

Something's going down. I can feel it.

Shamoun stood up first, threw some euros on the table, and the rest followed him outside as if they had been sucked out by a vacuum. Robert trailed not far behind as he watched them pile into a white van across the street. He was now glad he had taken the bike all the way to St. Denis instead of the metro. He mounted the seat, started it up and pulled out into traffic about five cars behind the van.

Twenty minutes later, the van was zig-zagging between the 17th and 18th Arrondissements of Paris and then barreled down Boulevard Haussmann. Robert could feel that something was happening and the adrenaline was surging through his veins, making his head tingle. Suddenly, the van pulled over to a stop a half-block from Galeries Lafayette and the sliding door opened, pouring out masked men like cockroaches coming out of a crack in the wall.

Robert quickly ditched his motorcycle and broke into a trot as he heard the clack of AK-47 fire and saw a cop fall down in the street. He approached the van first, popping two rounds into the passenger's head, and shooting the driver before he could react. He ripped open the door, using the passenger's body as a shield, and looked inside. Shamoun was backing away with one hand on the back door handle and the other on the trigger of his gun, which was pointed at Robert. In a split second, Robert dispatched him with a shot to the head and chest as Shamoun's gun went off, shattering the windshield. Technically that ended the assignment, but not for Robert. He was in combat mode. He grabbed an AK 47 from the floorboard of the van and took off toward the mall. The terrorists had to be stopped.

A uniformed police officer jumped in front of Robert on the sidewalk and raised his gun.

"Halt!"

Robert dispatched him with a shot to the head. As the officer fell to the ground like a lifeless rag doll, Robert ran around him and into the gallery, where he could hear screaming and shots being fired. He quickly bounded up the stairs, where he had a vantage of the entire sales floor, which had turned into a battlefield. Terrorists were shooting shoppers left and right, bodies crashing into glass sales counters as dozens of terrified people hit the floor in fear. Several in the crowd gave in to their flight impulses and ran. As they did, they were mowed down by machine gun fire.

Crouching low at the edge of the mezzanine, which was open to the main floor like a theater, Robert scanned the room for terrorist targets, one by one, counting them quickly and then carefully taking aim and shooting them like ducks in a shooting gallery.

"That's one," he called out to himself as he aimed, fired and a masked jihadist hit the floor. "Two!" He fired a spray of automatic fire at another masked man, downing him.

"Seven more to go."

Robert moved along the perimeter of the floor, changing positions and taking the terrorists by surprise, confusing them and making them believe there could be more than one shooter. He shot at them from one position, and then, crouching low, out of their sight, moved to another position around the circular floor, shooting and taking return fire from the terrorists.

He crawled backwards, taking cover behind a sales counter in women's wear as the object of the terrorists' wrath turned on him instead of the innocent shoppers, whom they were now taking as human shields instead of shooting them. This was not part of his assignment and every second he stayed on the scene increased his chances of getting caught. He took aim carefully and fired at the head of a terrorist wielding a woman shopper, and watched the shot connect as the jihadi fell, spraying random gunfire, and the woman scrambled away.

Bullets were exploding all around him, reminding him of his days in Iraq and later, in Syria. He stayed flat to the floor and crawled backwards as the bullets pocked and shredded the edge of the mezzanine and pinged against the wrought iron railing, creating clouds of white dust as they chipped away at the floor like a buzz saw. Mannequins riddled with bullets disintegrated into clouds of white powder as the clothes hanging on them fell. Display racks fell apart in a heap of dresses, pants and jackets as if they had been hit by wild gusts of wind.

Robert regrouped quickly, as he knew the terrorists would be fast approaching him from both sides. The mezzanine was round, like the rotunda itself, so there would be no escaping them. Whether he went left or right, he would still have to cross their path, and was sandwiched between them. He would have to make his stand. The element of surprise was with him because, since they were on their way up the staircase, the terrorists would not know his exact position. He heard them firing wildly on automatic as they bounded the steps.

He scooted into a changing booth, broke open the false ceiling, and perched himself on top of the structure, breaking out more ceiling tiles with a sweep of his weapon so he could see on both sides. From his hiding place inside the false ceiling, Robert took the approaching group on the right by surprise with a sweep of automatic fire. Two of them fell and the third took cover, firing back at him. He felt a singe of pain in his leg and then a feeling like it was on fire. He had been hit.

He couldn't afford to concentrate on the shooter because the group to his left probably already knew his position, so he turned his attention to them, spraying them with fire, scattering them as two dropped to the ground and Robert took another hit in the shoulder. He jumped down from his perch, his one leg numb and the other bending so he could lay flat and crawled toward his aggressor on the right, from whom he was still taking fire. As the bullets whizzed past him, Robert took aim at the jihadi's head, fired and watched it explode.

He turned and fired in the direction of the others on the left. They remained still as he crawled toward them. He saw that two were dead and a third man was moaning. He shot him in the head and saw the fourth man limping away and attempted to shoot him as well, but wasn't sure if he had connected or not. Through the commotion downstairs, he could hear sirens in the distance. That meant the whole mess would be someone else's problem now. He crept out through the causeway to the men's store and dragged his body away.

CHAPTER TWENTY-FOUR

Chaos reigned on Boulevard Haussmann as dozens of police cars and heavy equipment rolled up to the scene where frantic shoppers escaping were thrust into throngs of lookers-on. Dozens of armored cops poured out of a SWAT van and ran into the store in formation as shoppers fled. Already, the Twitter-sphere was full of smartphone videos posted by hip shot journalists. As the videos piled up on Instagram and Facebook and the tweets multiplied, social media was recreating a monster, bringing a legend back to life. The #Paladine hashtag resurfaced, referring to the lone shooter as a super hero, a savior.

Robert had first come to the public light when he had shot a terrorist at a McDonalds in the States, thereby saving dozens of lives. That is how he had picked up the "Paladine" moniker. Now, with the hundreds that had been saved from terrorists by the mysterious sniper in Galeries Lafayette, the new pundits of social media were recalling the event and declaring that France now had its own "Paladine," a hero who was dedicated to saving the world from terrorism.

Nobody called Inspector Nicolas Soussier to the scene. He was alerted by one of his men who had seen the news on Twitter and thought he may be interested in the "Paladine" angle. He was.

"You think it was our guy?"

"Too close not to check it out. Keep two men on the apartment and meet me at the crime scene."

They rolled out one unit to join the Inspector and the other one remained in surveillance of Robert's apartment.

Triage centers had already been set up on the sidewalk to evaluate the wounded and they were already in operation with dozens of casualties. There was no official death count yet, but the news was reporting hundreds saved rather than dozens killed. The Islamic State's brilliant terrorist attack on the infidels had been foiled.

Gregory Manizek's people were denying all knowledge of the incident to the French government while at the same time he was sending encrypted messages to Washington. Even he didn't know what was going on.

Two blocks from the violent scene, Robert collapsed in an alley, and crawled behind some debris as a cover. The blood had soaked through the makeshift tourniquets he had fashioned for his femur and shoulder. He had lost a lot of blood and his heart was pumping overtime to distribute what was left to his brain, shutting down the supply to the muscles that had propelled him this far, and despite his adrenaline-charged flight instinct, he could no longer walk. He dialed a number from his burner phone.

"Need help."

"Can you make it to the safe house?"

"Negative, I need, need..." Robert coughed. "Extraction. And don't fuck it up this time."

"What's your location?"

Robert looked up. The universe was spinning around his head. The voice on the phone became a distant echo. His sight was converging into blackness like the end of a Looney Tunes cartoon.

"GPS it."

"Hold on, we'll send someone right out."

He couldn't hold on. He was cold and shivering. There was a ringing in his ears. His limp hand fell to the ground and the phone clattered out to his side.

***

Arriving on the scene, Inspector Soussier flashed his badge, stepped through the yellow crime scene tape and entered the store. Bodies of shoppers lay on the ground all over the first floor. The copper scent of blood hung thick in the stuffy air, along with an alcoholic smell of perfume from the bursted bottles. He choked, almost gagged. Glass lay scattered all over the floor from the shattered jewelry and perfume counters, cases and windows. He approached a Sergeant on duty.

"Do you have a body count?"

"Yes, sir. 16 dead plus nine terrorist suspects."

"Nine terrorists?"

"Yes, sir."

"Show me."

Soussier toured the scene, mounting the stairs where Robert had made his last stand with the remaining terrorists.

"From the videos, it appears the shooter was up there."

The Sergeant pointed to the fitting room, on the floor of which was an ample pool of blood.

"When the crime lab gets here, I want them to test the DNA samplings of this blood against all the other victims – terrorists too."

"Yes, sir."

Soussier climbed the stairs, and stood next to the shredded changing booth, looking out into what had been Robert's theater.

***

The aide wiped his brow as he rushed to Nathan Anderson's office with the report, hoping he could get there before Anderson spotted the news. In the era of social media reporting, there was no need to wait for newspapers or broadcasts. News was in real-time and it was playing out on telephones and iPads all over the world almost immediately as it happened. When the aide opened the door, Anderson was sitting there with a frown. The aide held the binder out to his boss.

"I suppose this is a report on PAL?"

"Yes, sir."

"What's your name, son?"

"Gordon Allen, sir."

"Allen, who has the most sophisticated data gathering facility in the world, that's open 24 hours a day?"

Gordon shifted his weight on one foot. He looked puzzled. "We do, sir."

"That's right. So why am I reading about PAL on my phone instead of a report which should have been on my desk twenty minutes ago?"

"My apologies, sir."

Anderson held out his hand and Gordon put the folder into it. Anderson opened it, ignoring Gordon, who backed out of the office slowly.

"Wait a minute?"

"Yes, sir?"

"I want a full briefing on what Ted Barnard is given and what his next move is with PAL. The president will want to know."

"Yes, sir."

***

Soussier made notes and sketched in his pad as he walked the scene of the attack. He studied the videos that had been posted on the Internet. None were clear enough to positively identify Robert as the mysterious shooter. Yet, all the evidence, taken as a whole, was tearing at his gut. He didn't just suspect – he knew Garcia was Paladine. The challenge was convincing a judge to issue a warrant. He just had to rip this place apart and find something to connect him to these crimes.

You're pretty clever, aren't you, Paladine? Well I'm going to get you, and that's a promise.

CHAPTER TWENTY-FIVE

An unmarked white van appeared at the entrance of the alley and slowed beside a street bum lying next to a pile of garbage. The sliding door opened and two men stepped out, scooped up the seemingly lifeless homeless man and lifted him into the van. A third popped out of the passenger side door and swept up the garbage, the phone, and anything else that was in the immediate vicinity of his body into a black plastic trash bag and took it away.

Inside the van, the two attendants began working on Robert Garcia. They lifted him onto a backboard, cut away his clothes and the tourniquets he had made to locate the entrance and exit wounds, and applied pressure bandages. One attendant hooked up monitors to take Robert's vital signs, and the machine beeped to life, pumping out a weak pulse and a dangerously low blood pressure. Another put an oxygen mask to his face, opened up his eyelids and shone a light into his eyes. They moved quickly inside the rolling vehicle as it sped away, locating a vein and punching in a stint for the IV, which they hooked to the plastic flask of fluid swinging above the gurney.

***

Inspector Soussier pounded loudly on the door to Robert's apartment. Convinced there would be no answer, he completed the protocol nevertheless. Soussier was a man who always played the game by the book. Finally, after three token efforts, he gave a nod to the locksmith, who opened the door with a modicum of effort. Following Soussier, the search team scrambled inside the apartment like a colony of intruding ants.

At Soussier's direction, they pulled up the mattress in the bedroom, turned pockets inside out in all of Robert's pants and jackets, and emptied all his drawers to examine all of the contents.

"The bedroom is clean, sir. There's nothing here."

"Check the closet for secret panels."

One of the officers shone his flashlight inside the closet, examining every part of it carefully.

"Nothing."

They moved on to the bathroom, which was too small for the entire team, so Soussier delegated it to one officer, and accompanied the others to the living room and adjoining kitchen. There, every piece of furniture was upturned, the couch pillows extracted and examined, and even the armchair cushions, which were removable canvas covered pillows, were removed.

"Nothing here, sir."

A voice from the kitchen chimed out, "And nothing in the kitchen."

There was no computer equipment, no weapons, nothing of any kind which could connect Robert with either of the two murders they were investigating.

"Let's examine *le cave*."

The elevator to the basement was hardly big enough for two people, so Soussier rode it with the concierge to the basement floor. The rest of his search team took the stairs. When the doors opened on the dimly lit, dirt-floored basement, Soussier got a whiff of mildew which had taken hold of the wooden doors and remained there for years. His men were already waiting for him in the corridor, and the concierge led them all to Robert's storage unit. Soussier thanked the concierge for her help as an officer with a heavy pair of bolt cutters snapped the shank of the thick brass padlock and it hit the dirt with a heavy thud. They illuminated two bright battery powered lights and adjusted their beams upon the interior of the locker.

One by one, every item was removed and examined. An old golf bag, which turned out to contain nothing but clubs, stacks of musty magazines, space heaters, and bottles comprising a halfway decent wine collection. Soussier caught the policeman who was moving the bottles examining the labels.

"What are you doing?"

"I'm sorry, sir. I'm French, you know."

"We're all French here. We're looking for evidence, not the next good Bordeaux."

One of Soussier's team finally threw up his hands and made his report.

"There are no weapons here, sir."

"Are you sure we've searched everything?"

"Yes, sir. No guns, no weapons of any kind."

"He must have moved them."

"Well, they're not here."

"Alright, let's find him. Check with every hospital, veterinarian, and dentist in the area. Put the pressure on."

"What area, sir?"

"The entire city of Paris. That son of a bitch has to be here somewhere."

CHAPTER TWENTY-SIX

Billy Joel belted out "We didn't start the fire," while a rhythmic beeping sound kept time with it. A blinding, brilliant light, like the first dawn's sunlight through a window, increased in intensity, getting brighter and brighter until it stung Robert's eyes. They flickered open and he looked up at a plain white ceiling. Feet were shuffling all over. He tried to move, but found himself bound. He was weak, thirsty. He tried to speak through the oxygen mask. His throat was parched and scratchy.

He heard muffled conversation. "He's awake."

A face appeared above him, covered with a hairnet and below the smile dangled a surgical mask.

"You're a very lucky man."

Robert didn't feel lucky. He felt trapped, uncertain, but he was alive, and that was a good thing. He didn't know if he was being tended to by the good guys or the bad guys, relative terms in his business, labels of opinion that didn't reveal the shades or degrees of "goodness" or "badness."

"When can I get out of here?"

"Whoa, whoa. You've been shot in the shoulder and leg. The bullets missed major arteries, but they bounced around quite a bit and messed some things up. You've had surgery on your shoulder to repair damaged tissue, and you have a hairline fracture of the femur."

"Sounds like medical bullshit to me, doc. And it didn't answer my question."

"You should be in the hospital for about a week, then, depending on your physical therapy, I'd say you'll be up and around on crutches in three."

"Wonderful."

Robert closed his eyes and dozed off. Suddenly, he felt the sensation of movement. He heard automatic doors opening and then he saw flickers of successive ceiling can lights as they wheeled the gurney through the hospital corridor. He looked up at the nurse, whose large breasts, despite their containment, were flopping around under her non-sexy white smock as she pushed him into the elevator. The elevator hummed and bumped to a stop, the doors opened, and she pushed the gurney out and into a room and closed herself inside. Over the next few minutes, she and another nurse feverishly and methodically hooked up monitors and checked his IV drip. Nurse "Big Boobs" released his restraints and showed him the call button and the bed adjustment. Then, both of them left the room and Robert dozed off again.

When Robert opened his eyes again, he reached for the bed control and raised the head of the bed. It was then he became aware, for the first time, he was not the only one in the room. Sitting in the corner was the man with no name himself.

"If you had followed instructions, you wouldn't be here."

"Hello to you, too. Don't worry, there's no extra charge for the other eleven jihadis."

"What about the cop you wasted?"

"Collateral damage."

Manizek shook his head with disgust. "What did I tell you? Didn't I say to follow your instructions explicitly? There was only one target. You really fucked this one up."

"Then you would have been fine with a massacre of hundreds of civilians at Galeries Lafayette?"

"That's a French problem. Now it's just a mess. Not only that, Paladine is all over the Internet again. I should just wash my hands of all this and let the French have you."

Robert shrugged with his good shoulder. "Go ahead."

Manizek leered, surprised. "Go ahead?"

"You heard me. I stopped giving a shit a long time ago."

Manizek thought in silence for a moment. "You've made this my problem, so this time, and only this time, I'm going to clean it up. We can't have an international incident over this."

"An international incident? You mean like the war in Iraq? Weapons of mass destruction? Benghazi? Libya?"

Manizek ignored him. "We have to get you out of here."

"Doc said I'd be here for a week."

"No way. Too hot. You're bugging out today."

"What do you mean? I'm done."

"You're not done. There's one more remaining on your contract."

"What, you can't count?"

"You don't get credit for those other assholes you took out. Only the target."

"That's bullshit."

"Whatever. I don't have time to wipe your nose now. Just get over it. We have to get you out of here."

"Where am I going?"

"The where is figured out, and it's classified. The how, well, we're still working on that."

Without any further word, the man with no name stood up and walked out the door.

"Hey, wait!"

Nobody answered. Robert pressed his call button and, almost immediately, a nurse came running in.

"Tout va bien?"

"Yes, everything is fine. The man that just left, is he still out there?"

"What man, monsieur? We didn't see any man."

"You didn't see the man who was in my room?"

"No, monsieur. You haven't had any visitors."

The man with no name was, apparently, a ghost. Just like Robert.

CHAPTER TWENTY-SEVEN

Nicolas Soussier didn't have any evidence that Robert had been involved in the Galeries Lafayette attack, but it didn't prevent him from looking for him. He set up a dragnet all over Paris to find and detain Robert for questioning. His men made inquiries at every police station, hospital and morgue in the city. But it was the overreaching arms of the United States government, the ones that can extend themselves through the gaps of any net, that shielded him from Soussier's inquiries. The hospital Robert was in was no ordinary one. It was a very small facility, a safe house in its own right. There were no records, no reports, and nobody knew it even existed. The outside of the hospital appeared to be an ordinary warehouse in a grimy *banlieue* of Paris, not far from the *Charles de Gaulle Aeroport.*

At 10 p.m. a truck rolled up to the warehouse and backed to its loading platform. An attendant pulled the roll-up door and swung an inside door open, revealing what looked like a duplicate of Robert's hospital room. A nurse rolled Robert into the truck on a gurney and locked it into place on a special track in the floor of the vehicle.

"Aren't you coming with me?"

The nurse laughed and squeezed his hand. 'Not me, but someone else will."

"I'll bet she won't be as pretty as you."

The nurse smiled and waved to Robert as the attendant swung the large interior door closed. From the outside, this door contained a 3x5-foot faux mini-warehouse, chock-full with construction materials. Packed convincingly in the back of it were cut edges of drywall which looked like stacked sheets.

Anyone who opened the roll-up door to snoop around would see the building materials and never suspect the truck was a mobile hospital.

Robert's pain meds had started to wear off, but he didn't call for more. They put a dull edge on his senses. He wasn't used to putting his life in someone else's hands and he didn't trust Manizek at all. As the pain came rocking back, Robert greeted it like an old friend – a reminder he was still alive.

Five hours later, Robert felt the truck come to a stop. The attending nurse, who had hardly paid attention to him, announced they had arrived.

"Where?"

"We're very close to Metz. You will recover here."

***

Francois massaged Robert's leg vigorously and pushed it toward his torso, stretching the muscle. Robert wasn't homophobic, but he was tired of this touchy, feely nonsense from the muscle-bound therapist.

"Francois, no offense, but I can't take this physical therapy shit anymore. I need to work out myself before all my muscle turns to fat."

"But *Monsieur Robear,* you have been shot..."

I know that, you dolt.

"...You cannot run before you walk. You cannot fly before you have your wings...You..."

"I get it, I get it. But can we move up to the next level already? I don't have time to sit around."

"Monsieur, you are not sitting around. Physical therapy is a process. The body needs to heal."

Robert groaned and made a face, then motioned his head toward the multi-purpose weight machine in the room.

"Why don't I saddle up on that horse over there and give it some process?"

"I'm afraid your leg is too weak and your shoulder cannot take the pressure of the *resistance.*"

"I've got two shoulders and two legs, you know."

"I guess you could work the other two a little, but you must *promesse* not to strain yourself."

Robert felt like a kid. "I promise, Francois."

Cross my heart and hope to die.

"It is good for the cardiovascular *systeme* on the one hand, but on the other, there is the *probleme* of muscle imbalance."

Robert swung his legs off the bed, feet on the floor. "Let's try it without the crutches this time."

"No, Monsieur *Robear,* it is much too early."

"You said the quicker I get to walking, the better. Let me stand at least."

Francois nodded, and helped Robert to stand. He put a crutch under each armpit.

"How about just one?"

Robert gave the second crutch back to Francois and propped himself on the one under his left shoulder.

Lucky I got shot on both sides.

***

Ted Barnard had been avoiding Nathan Anderson. He had to think of a spin for the Galeries Lafayette covert operation. Potentially, both of their heads were on the chopping block and they had to get their stories straight for the president. Barnard passed the buck to the man with no name.

"Greg, what the fuck happened? One guy was supposed to disappear and now we've got a potential incident."

"Ted, don't worry, I've got everything under control."

"We can't afford our asset to be compromised."

"Everything is under control."

"Good, because if he gets rolled up we're screwed."

"It's taken care of."

Barnard hung up the phone, confident he could fill Anderson in and smooth things over. The man with no name was an expert in stage management. Barnard never questioned his methods because they always achieved results. And he didn't care (or dare) to know how they got done.

CHAPTER TWENTY-EIGHT

The more time he spent cooped up, the more he felt like a prisoner. He was not much of a reader, so the offer of books to read didn't interest him much. He didn't like television – whatever was on it was usually stupid and the news was always filled with fake news and propaganda, although in France it was a little better than in the States. Through his window he would look out at the Moselle River and wonder what it would be like to ambulate the streets of the 3,000-year-old town, if he could only walk. Above anything, Robert was fascinated with history; especially military history; and Metz had a ton of it. He promised himself to get off his crutches and evade his captors long enough to get a decent tour of the old walled Gallic Roman city.

Every day, Robert forced himself out of bed and walked to the window and looked out onto the river and the rest of the town, longing to feel it with his own feet. As he worked out on the weight machine, he felt himself becoming stronger and stronger as time passed. Finally, he couldn't stand it any longer. He had to get out.

Robert had medical caretakers, not keepers. There were no locks on his door. He could simply walk out of there, so he did. He waited for nightfall, and then left his room. The apartment was quiet. Only one attendant was on duty, and he was there mainly for logistics. Robert passed by the living room and saw the man asleep in a chair in front of the television. He slipped by him and into the foyer, where he rummaged through the coat closet. He found what he was looking for – a light coat – a little long for him, and baggy, but it would be perfect for what he had in mind. He draped the coat over his shoulders and slid the crutch under his arm and buttoned the coat over it in front, concealing the extra appendage. From his powers of observation he knew exactly where they kept the keys. He opened the small drawer in the foyer table and extracted them. Two seconds later, he was out the door. It was too simple.

Robert wandered the deserted narrow stone streets of the old town. A restaurant named *L'Escalier* had closed but the lights were still on. The busboy was stacking up the chairs inside that had spent the entire day on the street. A middle-aged guy was leaning against the wall, smoking. He passed by two girls on the corner who were chatting and paid him no mind.

Robert imagined these same streets that now tried to accommodate automobiles filled with horses and carts. New technology had come with the internal combustion engine, but the streets had stayed the same. One century colliding with the next. He continued meandering through the narrow streets toward a gold glow in the distant sky. He navigated toward the source of light. When he turned the next corner, the glowering spires of a massive gothic cathedral bathed in light revealed itself as the source.

CHAPTER TWENTY-NINE

After two weeks, there was finally a break in the monotony. As he was accustomed to in the military, before daybreak, Robert was awakened and told he was leaving by car to Munich. From there, he would take a series of trains to Istanbul. Another man with no name, although much lower on the food chain, supplied him with his transportation as well as his new identity, complete with passport and a tourist visa to Turkey. Even with the new credentials, air travel was too risky due to facial recognition software.

The driver with no name also proved to have the same when it came to personality. He was like a robot. That suited Robert just fine. He had nothing to say and wasn't about to make anything up just for the sake of useless conversation. He sat silently in the passenger's seat, looking out the window and listening to the hum of the engine and the faint rumble of the tires against the road.

The crack of thunder, a blinding flash of light and the spatter of rain against the windshield woke Robert from a light sleep. He opened his eyes to the rhythmic flapping of the wiper blades and could see a large storm front looming in the distance, periodically crackling with bolts of lightning. He glanced over at the driver, who was peering through the downpour. The rain pelted the car in torrents and the driver slowed, straining his eyes to see the road ahead and turning an eye to Robert, who showed him no sympathy.

"Do you want to stop for a bite to eat, perhaps?"

Robert thought about it, then it appeared that the guy was still alert, so he politely declined. He couldn't bear the thought of sitting silently with this zombie at a cafeteria table.

"I'll grab something at the train station."

"Suit yourself."

When the door opened at the train station in Munich, he finally felt his independence. For the last two weeks he had felt like he was in jail. He cruised the station, looking for something to eat, but the only things that seemed to be for sale at that hour were hot dogs. He ordered two with a plate of fried potatoes at the station's cafeteria. He picked up the hot dog, wondering why they were so popular there.

Germans must love hot dogs. But why make a fuss out of it, and so many different kinds? A tube steak is a tube steak.

He waited without incident, though not without worrying. Anything could happen at any time. He circled several times around the station to make sure he was not being followed. When he was relatively sure it was safe, he hung out in a different part of the station, well away from the track for his train to Zagreb.

At last call, he proceeded to board the train to Zagreb, which left Munich at 11:36, while looking about for any signs of a tail. Like all the trains in Germany, it left on time. For Robert, nothing, not even a train ride (especially that) was simple. His natural paranoia, combined with the artificial paranoia of having seen so many "tragedy on train" movies, from *Murder on the Orient Express* through *Silver Streak*, demanded that he sleep lightly, with one eye open, even though he had a private sleeper car all to himself. But travel fatigue, combined with the darkness out the window and the gentle rumbling of the train put him to sleep right away, and he didn't wake up until the porter announced their imminent arrival.

The next train from Zagreb to Belgrade was a little more interesting because it was daylight and he could look out the window. But being cooped up in the train was beginning to make him stir-crazy, like he had been during his recovery. This trip was a little more troublesome because it was only second-class, so Robert had to put up with neighbors. When one of them, an Englishman, tried to speak to him, he feigned ignorance, claiming he didn't speak English. The Englishman turned his nose in disbelief, but it suited Robert just fine. He wasn't a tourist and wasn't there to make any friends.

They had reserved an entire four-sleeper compartment for Robert for the overnight trip from Belgrade to Sofia, where Robert was stuck for a day waiting for the night train to Istanbul.

CHAPTER THIRTY

Crossing over into Turkey was like entering another planet. Spread out over Europe and Asia, which was only a bridge away, Istanbul was a city on two continents. Robert's transport, another silent type, this time a Turk, drove him in a small van, deep into the heart of the old districts, which were on the European side. The walls of the ancient city of Constantinople which had withstood the test of time, and its old mosques with their towering minarets showed the contrast of an ancient place against the stark background of modernity of one of the most heavily populated cities of the world.

The van came to a stop at an apartment in the *Sultanahmet* District, the oldest part of town.

"This is where you live."

The driver handed Robert an envelope, and he ripped open the top and spilled a set of keys into his hand. He opened the door, grabbed his backpack from the backseat, and said goodbye to the man of few words.

The apartment was small, but livable. Robert had never called a place home for more than a few months. He wondered if he would stay long enough at this one to develop any habits. He thought about his dog. They said they would "take care of it," but he had seen first-hand how "they" take care of things and it didn't give him comfort. But he knew that Marie, the caretaker, loved the dog and treated it as one of the family. Whenever his involuntary servitude was up, he vowed to return for him. For the time being, however, everything was shrouded in secrecy, including his identity and the mysterious new (and last) job they were saving for him.

***

The orchestra played "Hail to the Chief" as the president took the stage at the Annual White House State Dinner in a huge tent that had been set up on the White House lawn. This was the chance for Washington elite's who's who to rub elbows with the most influential power brokers in the world. As the president toasted Chinese President Xi Jinping in his own unique, late-night talk show host style, Nathan Anderson motioned to Ted Barnard across the table. Barnard understood it to be a call for an impromptu spy summit as soon as the president had finished speaking and the black-tie attendees went back to their Colorado lamb with fried milk and baby broccoli. Both men were hardly noticed as they excused themselves from the table at staggered intervals and met in an enclave near the men's room. To Barnard, Anderson was like a pesky fruit fly you tried to swat away but kept coming back. But he had the ear of the president and this had allowed him to insert his nose into this aspect of the company business.

"Has the PAL situation cooled off yet?"

"Everything is under control."

They both suddenly fell silent as two Chinese men exited the restroom. Barnard, slipping back into the role of head spy, put a hand on Anderson's elbow as he watched the two disappear.

"Good, because the next project is extremely sensitive. The president wants our best man on it."

"God man, you think PAL is our best man? He's a wild hair, a liability."

"Sometimes it helps to use your brain instead of just blindly executing orders. Besides, this assignment is so dangerous it borders on impossible. And there's nobody else who has proven that effective against the impossible."

"We can't afford a screw-up on this one."

"The man wants PAL, what can I say? Will he be ready or not?"

Barnard reluctantly nodded. "He'll be ready."

***

Two weeks had gone by without a word from them. Robert spent his days wandering around the old town, and buying his staples in the open market. His favorite time was the morning, when a thick blanket of low fog often covered the entire city, and he could walk around freely without having to worry that anyone was following him.

Robert became fascinated with the Galata Bridge. Every day, as part of his rehabilitation routine, he would walk from the old town across the top of the bridge to Asia, and commune with the fishermen at the rail, who seemed to always be there, hanging over the edge, with their fishing poles, smoking *nargile* water pipes and munching on fresh *givrek* from the baker's baskets: big, loopy donuts covered with sesame seeds. Or watching the *balik-ekmek* boats bobbing in the Golden Horn. Like elaborate gold-domed pagodas on top of carved hulls, the gaudy boats reminded him of piñatas, with their ridiculous bow figureheads of dragons or mermaids and their elaborate gold columns and swinging red and gold Ottoman lanterns. Robert was an expert at being anonymous, so it wasn't long before he was dressing, walking and talking like the rest of the crowd on the bridge, which also had its fair share of tourists.

Most days he'd walk back on the bottom level of the bridge, listening to the colorful cooks advertising their fresh fish sandwiches.

"Balik-ekmek, balik-ekmek!"

Robert watched a cook dressed in a red embroidered Ottoman costume on one of the boats stuff a generous load of grilled fish into a fresh half-loaf of bread and hand it to a customer. He walked along the bridge, being solicited by waiters in the restaurants.

"Balik-ekmek! Buyrun! Buyrun!"

He sat down at a table and, moments later, a smiling waiter brought him a steaming hot grilled fish sandwich, stuffed with mackerel, peppers and lettuce. Robert thanked him in Turkish.

"Teskur ederim."

The waiter bowed and smiled. *"Rica ederim.* Drink?'

"Yes, thank you. *Teskur ederim."*

The waiter came back with a glass of *salgam*, a drink made from fermented purple carrots, turnips and boiled wheat. It tasted kind of like pickle juice with the dominant taste being turnips. Robert liked it right away, probably because it was as strange as he was.

The daily trip across the bridge and back became a routine he looked forward to. He would buy fresh mackerel, angler fish or sea bream from the fish market vendors, who would clean the fish and wrap it in paper for him to take home. He thought he would get sick of eating fish, day in and day out, but soon began to daydream of having a boat himself. Being a hermit, Robert could definitely live on a boat, as long as it had a toilet, a shower and a galley. He'd saved up enough money from his earnings to live for years. Robert had never thought of retirement before. He had always thought he'd work until he got killed someday, and that would be that.

Maybe I should just chuck it all and stay here, change my name and hide in plain sight. They'd never find me and then someday they'd stop looking.

CHAPTER THIRTY-ONE

As Robert strolled the Galata Bridge with his latest fresh market purchases, he paused and hung over the rail, and watched an old fisherman next to him struggle with his catch and then bring a nice-sized sea bass home. The old man cut the line and pulled the hook out, and the fish flopped around inside his bucket. He squinted up at Robert, whose hands were loaded with paper, nodded and said something in Turkish. Robert responded in Arabic.

"I don't speak Turkish."

The man smiled and switched to Arabic. "I see you here every day, buying fish. Why do you buy when you can just catch it?"

Robert paused, thinking about it a second.

Why not?

"Where can I get my tackle?"

The man ran his fingers through his grey moustache. "I can help you. Come back here early tomorrow morning and we will set you up with everything you need."

From the following morning, Robert was fishing and learning how to speak Turkish. The man's name was Dimitri Galanos. He was a Greek who had lived in Istanbul for many years. The lines on his face were many, but Robert could read them like a palm reader. They told of a hard life, sadness and grief, but his warm smile and patient manner of fishing made it evident he had found his peace.

"I thought the Turks hated the Greeks."

"We have a rich history, like two fighting relatives. But people are people and we all need to live together and get along. Do the French hate the Germans?"

"I suppose not."

"Well?"

Robert spent most of his free time on the bridge, fishing alongside Dimitri. He was like the grandfather Robert never had. But the fishing was slow going. Robert had spent about a week and had nothing but nibbles on his line.

"I don't think I'm meant to do this."

The old man's white mustache raised in a warm smile, and he said in his gruff voice, "Son, just like no man was born a lawyer or an architect, no man was born a fisherman. When you learn to be patient, to treat time as relative and stop counting it like it's a bunch of beans, you will catch fish – so many you won't even be able to count them."

Robert tried to follow his advice.

"Hold the pole gently. Become a part of the sea. That way the fish will think your bait is just another fish for them to eat."

The Zen art of fishing.

Robert cast his line and relaxed on the bench.

"Think of the underwater world, *malaka*. You are a part of it now. Forget time. It is not your friend anyway."

Suddenly, Robert felt as if he had entered another world – him, Dimitri and the other fishermen at their sides. The regular world was buzzing on by, tending to their appointments, responsibilities. Life for them was moving at a rocket's pace. Even the tourists seemed preoccupied with their sightseeing schedules. Not the fishermen. They were happy just to be there, on the bridge, fishing. The old man put his hat over his eyes to take a snooze, holding his pole while he slept.

Robert felt a quiver on his line. 'Dimitri!"

Dimitri threw his hat off and looked up. "That's it! Tug on it gently. Make him think the little fish on your line is getting away."

Robert tugged and felt a pull on the line. Then, it started to unwind quickly, spinning, spinning.

"Good! Reel him in, *malaka*, reel him in!"

Robert pulled back on the pole reeling, and the pole bent forward like a tree branch heavy with winter snow.

"Don't let him get away!"

Robert reeled and reeled, pulled and pulled, until he saw the silver flash of a fish flying above the surface.

"That's a big one!"

Now, the other fishermen had all come to alert and were cheering him on, as if it was some kind of significant event. For them, it was. Robert struggled with the fish until he had exhausted it and brought it up to the pier, catching it with his net.

"That's the biggest sea bass I have ever seen on this bridge. Must be over a kilo!"

From that day on, fishing became a passion with Robert. He still bought fresh bread from the vendors at the bridge, but he caught so much fish he never had to buy another fish sandwich. As it was when he had lived in the Rocky Mountains, Robert's freezer soon became packed with frozen fish, stacked like plastic-wrapped bricks from floor to ceiling.

He found a gym to supplement and accelerate his recuperation efforts and worked it into his routine every day after fishing. The gym was not far from the bridge, so, after cleaning his fish, he would take it home, stow his equipment, put one fish in the fridge for dinner and the rest into the freezer, and then it was off for a vigorous two-hour workout.

Before long, not only was he walking without a recognizable limp, but building up to the same physical training routine he had before the shooting. Robert was ready to go back into action. He checked in daily with his PGP mail, and was pleasantly surprised to find a message from Lyosha.

Bob, I have been wondering why I haven't heard from you. I have been thinking to come back to Paris soon.

Without revealing his location, Robert responded that he had left Paris and didn't know how long it would be until his return.

The message from Lyosha made his mind wander to his holiday in Moscow, which they had so rudely interrupted. Robert had never had a significant close relationship with any woman, only a series of starts and stops, but it didn't mean he wasn't curious about how it would be. Lana was so soft and nice and her presence, even though it had been for just a few days, had made him feel good in a way he had not felt for a long time. He shifted his gaze to the burner phone on the table, one of three he had purchased, and activated it. From memory, he dialed her number.

"*Allo?*"

"Hello, Lana? This is Bob."

There was silence on the other end.

"Bob, do you remember me?"

"*Yes, Bob, of course I do. How are you?*"

There wasn't really anything he could tell her. He couldn't say: *Well, I killed two terrorists and that went okay but now the police are looking for me. But the third assassination didn't go so well after I offed eleven jihadis and got shot in the leg and the shoulder, but I'm okay,* so the conversation was a short one.

"Oh, I'm alright. I've been thinking about you lately."

"Really, why?"

"Because I really enjoyed the time I spent with you and always regretted that it was cut short."

Now he was regretting even this phone call. It was a mistake. He couldn't invite her to Istanbul to hang out with him while he hid from the French authorities and waited for his next kill assignment.

"Well, I'm still here in Moscow, and would be happy to see you any time."

That answer gave Robert a good feeling, like she was actually in the room with him. Acceptance was the only form of friendship he had ever known.

"Great, I look forward to it."

"Me too. And Bob?"

"Yes?"

"Call me again, will you?"

Robert agreed to do that, and hung up, feeling satisfied, but he had to abandon his fantasies for grim realities when he opened his PGP mail and found a message.

Personal meeting. Tomorrow, Taksim Gezi Park., 1300 hrs.

It wasn't signed, but Robert knew who it was from – the man with no name.

CHAPTER THIRTY-TWO

Mothers were rolling their babies in strollers and some young people were hanging out in the park, but it was otherwise empty. Robert approached a circular fountain surrounded by flowerbeds with colorful flowers. He sat down at the opposite end of a bench which was already occupied by a man reading a newspaper. His words fell on the man's ears in the pauses between rhythmic spouts of fountain water.

"Don't you know people don't read those anymore?"

"The hell you say?"

The man kept hold of the paper and didn't move his attention from it, as he removed a folder from his lap and slid it across the bench.

"Couldn't you have done this by PGP? What is it, your flair for the dramatic?"

"Not this one. This is top secret."

Robert smirked, grabbed the file and realized the man with no name was gloating at him as he lit up a cigarette.

"I was against you taking this job."

Robert opened the folder and flipped through it. "What else is new?"

"General Yaman Hemsani is the commander of the Syrian Arab Army Forces of the Basha al-Assad regime."

Robert held up his hand. "Wait a minute. Russia is in there actively supporting Syria with ground force training. Wouldn't a direct hit against a top Syrian general be an act of war against Russia, by proxy?"

"The sensitive nature of this makes it fall within our territory."

"You're talking about the assassination of a top military commander of a sovereign nation that we are not at war with."

The man with no name frowned. "How many times do you have to be instructed not to question your assignments? The president has made no secret of the fact that he supports regime change in Syria."

"By giving aid to rebel forces. But this is an act of war. There's no authorization for military force against Syria."

"This man has been sanctioned by the United States Treasury for human rights abuses. And he's supporting a criminal regime."

"Says you."

"Says the President of the United States."

"It's an overt act."

"It is an overt act for which the United States will claim no knowledge or responsibility. That's why you need to execute it and anyone who might get in the way of the target."

"I don't like it. This one really stinks."

"The only thing standing between you and life in prison or the needle is this one more job."

Robert stood up, leaving behind the file like it was a piece of garbage.

"But who knows whether you'd even make it to see your trial. Anything can happen."

Robert paused and turned.

"I'm not stupid enough to think I'd make it that far. You'd kill me off and invent some kind of bullshit story about it. But what makes you think I give a shit whether I live or die?"

"Just do the damn job, and all is forgiven."

"What about my exit?"

"It's all set up. Everything's there, in the file."

He took a drag of his cigarette, then flicked it with his index finger and it hit the sidewalk in an explosion of sparks. Without another word, he left the bench along with the deposit he had made, and walked away.

Robert thought about killing him right there and setting his body on the bench, posed like a mannequin reading the paper, crossing his legs for extra authenticity. He imagined himself putting a bullet in the man's head as he walked away. As the man with no name disappeared, Robert sat back down on the bench and regarded the file folder as if it was a rotten piece of stinking meat.

He stared at the dossier sitting on the bench as if it were worse than a pestilential virus; as if touching it would somehow infect what was left of his soul, if he ever had one. He was an atheist, of course, not one of those crusaders who believed he was killing in the name of God and country. He wasn't a believer in heaven, nor hell for that matter. As far as he was concerned, if hell did exist, it was right here on earth. What made man think he was any more significant than any other mass of protoplasm stimulated by electrical impulses? Why were we any better than the bugs we squash under our feet? If anything, we were worse. Surely the insects provided more benefit to the earth than we did. They recycled tons of waste. All we did was create it. They provided tons of food for birds and animals. All we did was eat and shit. We killed each other to get the other one's stuff, we killed animals for food, and we were the only ones who also killed them and each other just for fun.

To Robert's way of thinking, everything man touched was ruined.

What made us humans so special? What gave us the right to think we were the chosen race, above the monkeys and the lions, the tigers and turtles? Because we kill for no reason? Or for any reason? Because we'd thought of a way to kill everything on our planet with the push of a button? Or was it because there was so many of us, even if we never pushed that button, our destructive presence alone would wipe out every living thing on earth?

In the end, Robert was an instrument, not a philosopher. He lived by a code and that code was his religion. This was his *job*, and the purpose of his life was to perform it, not question it. He extracted a large wad of cash from the folder and shoved it into his pocket, and tucked the folder itself into his jacket.

***

The next day on the bridge was his last. As he sat next to Dimitri, he imagined building a life for himself there in Istanbul as the anonymous fisherman. But, unfortunately, it could never be. He watched as the old man cast out his line and settled back on the bench. Robert was not doing as well with his catch as usual.

"Something wrong, malaka?"

"How did you know?"

He motioned to Robert's empty bucket. "You're not catching any fish. Looks like you've lost touch with 'the force'."

"I have to leave."

"When are you coming back?"

Robert hesitated. "I'm not."

The old man nodded as if he had already known.

"I'm going to miss this place."

Dimitri put a hand on his shoulder and looked in his eyes. "Home is not a place, malaka. You can find the peace you have found here anywhere. Just remember what you've learned about fishing. Remember how many times the fish slipped off your hook and got away?"

"Yeah."

"And remember the days that were all like that – close calls, and you caught nothing?"

Robert nodded and smiled.

"But you didn't give up, did you?"

"No, I guess not."

"That's right. You kept up at it until you became as good a fisherman as any of us on this bridge. Sometimes it's the failures in life that define you, not the accomplishments. Plus they make the winning all the more sweet."

Robert nodded, understanding.

"So the next time you can put a pole in your hand, let your mind wander to this time, here. And, if at the end of the day, your bucket is full of fish and your mind is free, you will know that you are home."

CHAPTER THIRTY-THREE

Robert sensed something was off about Gaziantep. It was a large city, but not as big as Istanbul. It was chock-full of apartment buildings and mosques with picturesque protruding minarets, but there was a jihadist undercurrent to it that Robert could almost smell. Its proximity to the Syrian border made it the logical place for new recruits to meet their ISIS escorts and for sex traffickers selling women to the Islamic State. It also was a hub of the nefarious money exchange operations Robert had learned about when he was researching his hit on Naifeh. Gaziantep was only 11 hours from Istanbul by car but a world away culturally. In that respect, it was closer to its neighbor and sister-city Aleppo, only 60 kilometers away.

He waited in a café in the old section of town for his two Special Forces counterparts to show up. Their mission was to deliver materials and training aid to the Free Syrian Army, a name self-proclaimed by several different loosely organized bands of rebels whose self-declared mission was to fight Bashar al-Assad's rule of Syria. When two young men with cropped hair and wearing conspicuous tourist clothing showed up, he knew it had to be them.

They were both in their early 20s, - babies really –probably right out of live environment training, and too full of pride and testosterone. Both tall, one wore a baseball cap over his blonde crew cut and a white T-shirt and blue jeans. The other was in blue jeans and a print shirt that had "Turkey" written across it instead of the name of a sports team. They nervously looked around the café like it was their first time on the block, and it probably was. Failing to spot Robert, they sat down at a corner table, removed from all the patrons. Robert picked up his coffee cup and walked over to them. They both looked up at him in surprise as he sat down at their table.

"Mind if I join you gentlemen?"

They both looked up at Robert curiously. The blond spoke up first. "Actually, we're waiting for somebody."

Robert stared at them incredulously, eyebrows raised. "Aren't you going to ask me what the countersign is?"

The second one fired back, "What is the countersign?"

Robert frowned. "Sex. Really guys, could you be even more American? Why didn't you just dress in your uniforms?"

"Our orders were to dress like tourists."

"Like tourists or American flags?"

The blond piped up. "So we should dress like a bag of smashed asshole, like you?"

Robert stared him down and his face twitched when his partner kicked him under the table.

He was actually glad the young soldier had been rude. It meant they didn't know anything and the secrecy of his own mission was intact.

"Guys, I was a soldier once, just like you. We don't need to prove whose dick is bigger here. All I need from you is a short ride, so let's all try to get along, okay?"

That comment evoked smiles, even from the blond, and the frost was finally thawed. Robert reached his hand across the table. "Bob."

The brown-haired guy was the first one to shake his hand. "I'm Sergeant Bill Reeves and this is Sergeant Patrick Schofield."

Robert shook their hands with his vice-grip special. As they got to know each other over coffee, guards remained up but the mood became more civil.

"You're to meet us at the SP at o-seven-hundred. Have you got a pen?"

"Don't need one. Just give it to me."

Robert memorized the address, put money on top of the bill and left.

***

Robert reported early to the joint Turkish and U.S. command center and was issued the desert camouflaged uniform that the rest of the unit he was traveling with would be wearing, sans insignia, which suited him just fine, along with a duffle bag that contained indigenous clothing. He was also issued two cases which contained his "tools of the trade."

He joined up with Reeves right away and took a seat in his Humvee along with three other men, introduced to him as Lieutenant Samuel Peterson, Specialist Hamil Jordan and PFC Joe Walker. Robert sensed it wasn't the first rodeo for the three others and that they weren't too keen on their Reeves being as green as he was. He was just happy not to be travelling with Schofield.

They took off as part of a small convoy of military vehicles and brand new Toyota pickup trucks, and were soon crossing over into Syria through the Ocupinar Gate. The air was dead calm, with less dust and a whole lot cooler than it was during Robert's last time around. He figured it to be about in the mid-80s which was like sitting out by the swimming pool with an ice-cold lemonade compared to the blistering heat of July.

"So Bob, is this your first time to Syria?"

"Sorry, Lieutenant, I'm not allowed to tell that to anyone – it's classified – but from the looks of you I know you can figure it out."

"Yes, I think I can. So I suppose I don't have to tell you this whole effort completely sucks balls."

"How so?"

"You don't know?"

"Why don't you tell me?"

"Well, not knowing exactly what your mission is, I can only give you general advice and that's to watch your back."

Robert furrowed his brows, bewildered. "What do you mean?"

"I mean, sleep with one eye open if you can. Don't get me wrong – I'm not questioning my orders. I'm a soldier and I follow them. But nobody here on the ground believes in this mission. Almost half of these bastards we're training have defected to al-Nusra."

"I see."

"This is my second tour here and it's even worse than it was in Jordan."

"Have you reported this to your command?"

"Hell, yeah. Like I said, I don't question my place. We're just following orders, but it doesn't feel right, you know? We came here to fight terrorists, not teach them how to fight us, and that's what it feels like."

Robert could sense Reeves' enthusiasm was already waning.

"Plus now we've got the Russians running around."

"Russians?"

"Yeah, you see them around at the checkpoints and stuff. They're not in uniform, but you see 'em hanging out with the Syrian officers and you can tell they're Russians, all right."

Of course, Robert already knew about the Russians but there was nothing he could say about it. At that point, Walker couldn't help but chime in. "We've seen them in the air, too, sir."

"Yeah, we've spotted Russian drones all over the place."

"I suppose they're fighting ISIS, too."

"I guess. But they're also fighting the FSA, the Levant Front and the Army of Conquest – all these guys who we've been providing aid to. Makes you feel like we're smack dab in the middle of another cold war."

"War's never cold, Lieutenant. It's always hot."

Peterson smiled. "You're right about that, sir."

By the time they had arrived at Robert's drop point in the village of Azaz, the conversation had lightened and turned to women, something Robert had no input to provide. But, listening to the guys talk about their girls back home made his thoughts drift to Lana. She had always been out of reach, someone he could never have. Now she was also an enemy.

CHAPTER THIRTY-FOUR

Azaz was a blown-out shithole, similar to Aleppo, but a lot smaller. When they arrived at the checkpoint, Robert began to see for himself just what Peterson had been talking about. Being an expert in tracking down jihadis, he was astonished that the members of the Levant Front, the rebels who were operating the checkpoint, looked remarkably like the targets he had been stalking. He noticed it first when they stopped. The guards wore their socks pulled up past their ankles, almost halfway up to their knees, like they were wearing shorts or their camo pants were too short for their legs. It was *haram* to wear anything over the ankles, so the exposure of black socks gave them up as extremists right away. They wore their uniforms just like ISIS militants.

Robert hitched a ride in the cab of one of the Toyotas, in a group of seven headed for rebel-controlled eastern Aleppo. As they drove in formation toward the city, it reminded Robert of the jihadis who, driving the same type of Toyota pickup trucks, had attacked him the previous summer. He felt like he was riding with the enemy. But, this was his last assignment. After that, he'd buy a little sailboat with the money he had saved up, fish and live off the sea.

I'm definitely getting too old for this shit.

General Hemsani was a "hands-on" commander. Using the fresh Intel Robert had memorized from the file, he figured the general would not be too hard to find. The Syrian Army had established a base in the ancient Citadel. Perched on a 160-foot high hill and surrounded by a 72-foot deep moat, it was a site that Robert felt would be the most logical for a command center. Robert set out for the citadel on a one-man recon mission to locate the general and formulate a plan to kill him. He bought a Chinese motorcycle off one of the rebels and set off toward the old city.

***

Without the benefit of drone surveillance himself, he had to do it the hard way. Since the tallest structure near the citadel, the 1,000-year-old minaret of the Great Mosque, had been destroyed, he climbed to the top of the minaret of the nearby al-Atroush Mosque, which was only 200 meters south of the fortress, close enough to hit it with a golf ball. Crouched on the cool stone pavement of the uppermost floor, he surveyed the castle with field glasses. Robert had studied the citadel as part of his courses in military history when he was in the Army. It was one of the oldest castles in the world, protected by UNESCO, as was the old city surrounding it, which had been all but completely destroyed.

Upon its already formidable protective walls were machine gun emplacements, stacked with white sand bags. He also noticed several PRP-4A Argus reconnaissance vehicles with artillery placed in guard positions around the grounds in the old city, which confirmed to him the Russians were there or were at least supplying them. Despite the pounding the fortress had taken in the years of civil war, it still remained virtually impenetrable. But nobody was entering the fortress through the impressive bridge and main entrance complex.

How are they getting in there?

He sketched their comings and goings, and it appeared to him they must be using underground tunnels for access. He knew that the citadel had them.

The western gate had been destroyed by the same guys Robert was hanging with. Like the Carlton Hotel, which his compatriots had taken down in 2014, they had blown it up with the use of an underground tunnel network they had been working on for years to wage subterranean warfare against the Syrian government forces. The citadel wasn't the only culturally protected site destroyed in Aleppo. That and the defectors to al-Nusra Peterson had told him about gave him a very uneasy feeling. Robert was a killer, but he had always felt he had been on the right side. Now he felt like he was fighting with the terrorists instead of against them.

It was impossible to strike the interior of the fortress from anywhere in the city. That, and the fact that Robert didn't know the general's location or even if he was, in fact there, made this assignment the most complicated one he had ever been given. At nightfall, he left the mosque and rode back to base camp, determined to learn as much as he could about the citadel before he returned. Knowledge to him could mean the difference between life and death.

CHAPTER THIRTY-FIVE

Back in Azaz, Robert was able to hook his laptop up to wireless Internet provided through Turkish wireless services to the rebel camp. In addition to the regular Intel being fed to him by the man with no name, he found a wealth of information on the citadel from the Aga Khan's restoration project and tourist guides. From the documentation, Robert determined the two structures in which the general would most likely establish his command post would be either the old barracks, which had been converted into a visitors' center and museum, or the completely restored Mamluk Throne Hall which rested on top of the main entrance complex. From the rare but recent photographs he had seen of the throne hall, it appeared to be uninhabited and was lacking comparable facilities. A night attack on the visitors' center made the most sense to him, that was, if the general was even there. He memorized the floor plans of both structures and their locations within the fortress, as well as the general plan of the interior.

He finally received the confirmation he so badly needed when Manizek informed him that reliable intelligence showed that the general was, in fact, in Aleppo and had taken up headquarters in the citadel. Robert would enter the castle through one of the secret passages under the slope. Since it would be guarded, he would wear a protective mask and flood the tunnel with fentanyl gas. From there he would have to kill any guards at the other end of the tunnel and then do a fast recon on the visitors' center first and then the throne hall, if necessary, to determine the most likely command post location. Then, it would be an assessment of the opportunities to take the shot, and what hostilities he would likely face afterwards.

The most complicated part would be the escape route, since there were so many variables that were unknown. To cover his escape, he needed a diversion. Once at the visitors' center, he would cut the main power lines, sneak away as much as he could and fight the rest of the way out in the dark. If the way he came in was blocked, he would use another secret passageway below the throne hall to get away.

***

The following day, Robert was back into the Darknet, where he discovered another PGP mail from Manizek, which he assumed would be another one of his many Intel briefings. It was not.

FRAGO: You will execute the mission and be followed by a rebel breach team, who will assist you if necessary.

It was then Robert realized the general was not as important to them as the rebels breaching the citadel. He was the guinea pig they were sending in to pave the way for a rebel death squad to go in there, kill everybody and take the citadel for themselves. Not only would they capture key pieces of Russian military equipment, but also a strategic position in the city that would enable them to hold out should the Russian involvement increase.

Peterson was right. This does suck balls.

He typed a response: "This wasn't the agreement. You know I work alone. Request reassignment."

Robert slammed the top down on the notebook, clenched his fists and pounded one on the desk. He knew his request would be denied. His options were either to follow his orders and walk into a beehive full of killer bees, where the chances of getting killed were higher than he cared to estimate, face criminal charges back home, or try to disappear again.

"Shit! Shit! Shit!"

He paced the floor, hand to his head. There was only one thing in his crazy, lethal life that ever made sense. The code. He had to follow the code. Without the code there was nothing. This was his assignment. He had to carry it out, no matter what the consequences. If his number was up, it was up.

***

Ted Barnard dialed a secure, direct line to the man with no name. It rang and rang and rang, but finally Manizek picked up.

"Yes?"

"How'd he take it?"

"The little bastard's requesting reassignment."

"What did you tell him?"

"Nothing. I'm gonna let him sweat a bit."

"What if he doesn't do it?"

"He'll do it. Crazy fuckers like this guy live by some crazy unwritten law of the universe. It's the only thing that makes sense to them."

"And if he doesn't do it?"

"Then it will be Plan B."

"Plan B?"

"We send someone – just like him – to insure his silence."

Barnard knew what that meant, of course, but he didn't want to discuss the dirty details. That's what men like Manizek were for. The denials, if they need be given, could better be given with sincerity, and they could only be feigned if you didn't know them at all.

***

Robert checked his PGP, almost excessively. There was no response from the man with no name who had, until the day before, been feeding him a steady stream of Intel.

"Asshole."

He resolved to continue his planning as if the mission were going forward, but there was no way he was going to plan an invasion. He was responsible for himself and nobody else. Getting in, doing the job and getting out alive were the only three acts to this play.

Robert calculated the citadel was, most likely, occupied by at least a company of 80 to 100 soldiers. If it housed an entire battalion, he would be looking at 500 soldiers. They were sending him on a suicide mission. He didn't know how many "rebels" planned to invade the castle and he didn't care. Nobody talked to Robert about it. They understood his mission was classified and he wouldn't talk to them anyway. But they all seemed to be well aware he was the sacrificial lamb who would blaze the trail for their entrance. They were an annoying and dangerous variable to his plan that was impossible to calculate. There was no way to anticipate what may happen.

They watched Robert constantly, always keeping an eye on his comings and goings and constantly assessing his activities. It was beyond annoying and downright dangerous. Their commanders were constantly questioning him on his mission, but all they got was his usual response: "It's classified."

Robert was off every day early, scouting for his mission. Through his keen observation, he traced movements of Syrian Army soldiers through the streets on the western side of the city. There were armored vehicles parked alongside the rubble of the old Carlton and a bunch of soldiers hanging out around them, smoking cigarettes and holding radios. He observed supplies disappearing behind the plastic sheets covering a bombed-out store – soldiers and supplies going in and nothing coming out.

That has to be a secret passage.

CHAPTER THIRTY-SIX

Robert's daily recon trips to the city were becoming routine to his rebel neighbors. Now they formed the basis of a different goal – privacy. He couldn't afford to be shaking a tail of terrorists behind him every time he made a move, so he needed to outsmart them to get some distance from them. First, he located a suitable, abandoned building on the outskirts of the city. Inside, he made a makeshift underground locker for his equipment from the rubble. He dug a hole and put his equipment in it and covered the hole with stones, and booby-trapped it to ward off potential looters. Every day, Robert took several pieces of equipment and essential supplies with him to his new "storage space" so, when the time came, he wouldn't be leaving the rebels dressed like Rambo, alerting them to the onset of his mission. After a few days of transporting materials, he was ready. All in all, he had assembled an RPKN with night vision scope, an armor-piercing knife; a Glock 17 9mm pistol with noise suppressor; a helmet with night vision goggles; a gas mask; and a lightweight plate carrier vest. He loaded the pouches of the plate carrier with fully charged magazines and gas canisters.

Finally, Robert was ready. He set out on what looked like a regular, routine reconnaissance mission, with his RPK slung over his shoulder as usual, only this day he did not come back at nightfall as he normally would. He waited at his staging area until it was completely dark, then headed toward the unofficial front between all the fighting factions in Aleppo.

He hid his motorcycle in the rubble of an abandoned building and covered the rest of the trip on foot, slinking close to the buildings like a cat on the prowl. Hearing the rumble of a vehicle, he ducked behind a half-destroyed wall, hiding in the shadows as he watched a Syrian Army patrol in two infantry mobility vehicles pass by slowly. When he was sure they had gone, he once again advanced.

Dipping into a shelled-out building next door to the tunnel entrance, Robert suited up and slipped back out into the night. Outside the plastic sheeted "doors" of the store, he drew his Glock and silently dispatched the two sentries posted there, who both dropped like marionettes who had their strings cut with a dull, dusty thud.

He donned his mask and tossed a fentanyl canister inside the store, waited for it to take effect, and cautiously entered, spotting right away two more guards who had succumbed to the gas. Behind them was an opening in the floor leading to a set of stone steps going underground. He tossed another canister into the abyss. Once the gas had done its deed, he descended the steps into a dusty, muddy tunnel about six feet wide and only a slightly bit taller. He advanced carefully, about 100 meters, reaching a cut stone secret passageway to the citadel. The stone floor was smooth, having been worn and polished from hundreds or maybe thousands of years of traffic. The passage was tranquil, but for the shuffling of his own footsteps. After another 800 meters, Robert was standing at the bottom of a spiral staircase of stone, having met no more resistance up to that point. He detonated two gas canisters in the stairwell and, hearing nothing, began to mount them.

As he climbed, he saw the reflection of light at the top of the spiral stone staircase. Extending his spy mirror like a periscope, he panned the area, located two sentries on watch, talking to each other. He memorized their coordinates. Cautiously, he raised himself high enough to get his shooting arm free above the opening and took aim, shooting first one, then the other, with silent fire from his Glock, dropping both of them instantly. He climbed out of the stairwell and commandeered the usable weaponry of the two guards.

Robert was inside the citadel under a grand stone arch. He peered around one corner and then the other, noting the positions of the machine gunners at their lookout posts on the top of the ring wall. He knew they hadn't heard anything, because they were still looking out beyond the castle walls for intruders, unaware one was already among their midst.

He ran close to the walls of the excavated ancient barracks toward the visitors' center and museum. With any luck, the general would be there, and he could get in and get out before the entire Syrian Army scrambled after him. He patiently trekked in the shadows, crouching below the walls of the visitors' center, an old reconstructed barracks from the 1800s.

The first order of business was to set a charge to take out the electricity. Robert located the power box, loaded it with C4 explosives, and crawled back around the perimeter of the building. He paused below the first window, carefully extended his tactical spy mirror, and the light from the room gave him a decent view of everything inside. There were a couple of soldiers in the first room, drinking coffee. He crept on to the next window. Nothing there – so he moved on. There were fifteen windows in all to check, and he was running low on precious time.

Finally, when Robert got to window 14, he saw a familiar face, but it wasn't the general's – standing there with two other guys in Russian Spetsnaz dress was his old friend, Lyosha.

CHAPTER THIRTY-SEVEN

Robert shook off the initial shock. If Lyosha got in the way of his target, he would have to kill him – plain and simple. Lyosha would do the same thing in his place. If he discovered Robert was gunning after the general, he would take Robert out. Both men were on different sides now, but they lived by the same code. Robert waited patiently. The Russians weren't there just on vacation; the general couldn't be far behind. One of the Russians moved quickly toward the window.

Shit! He saw me!

Robert pulled the mirror down and lay flat on the ground beneath the window in the darkness. He could see the Russian's nose as he peered through the window, then, seeing nothing, left. Robert gingerly raised his periscope again, getting a good view of the players in the room. At that moment, the general walked through the door and stood by the Russians, talking.

Bingo!

Noting that his window of opportunity was somewhere between slim to none, Robert rose up and looked into the window long enough to take his aim and fire, twice, and the general went down.

The Russians were quick to react, two withdrawing their firearms and heading for the window while another jumped on top of the general's body to protect him. However, it was too late for the general. Robert's shots had found their purchase accurately, in the head and chest. Robert hit the button on the remote detonator and the entire citadel went dark. He couldn't go back to the tunnel unnoticed, because soldiers were pouring out of the visitors' center and taking positions outside, so he set out to traverse the citadel's grounds to the alternate escape route.

He had to cross one wide-open space between the visitors' center and the Mosque of Abraham, crouching down in the darkness as he heard random machine gun fire and screaming from all directions. He looked up and could see muzzle flash from the machine gun positions on the ring wall. They were randomly shooting into the citadel's grounds. He reached the beginnings of a street and lay flat outside the mosque. He could see the bouncing beams from the flashlights of soldiers running from the entrance complex toward the visitors' center.

Then, a series of loud explosions lit up the inside of the fortress. The citadel was under attack and he was stuck inside it. They obviously didn't care about blowing up things inside the ancient landmark.

The Russians were right. These are the bad guys.

It wasn't as if he could run up to the rebels and say, "Hey guys, I'm with you." The Syrians and the Russians would shoot him before he got to them and the rebels were likely to shoot him as well. He doubled back around the mosque and headed toward the hammam. With the map in his head, he had his bearings and with his night vision goggles, he was a ghost.

On the other side of the hammam, he reached the souk, and continued until he crept up on the entrance complex. There were a series of three gates, designed like a labyrinth to keep outsiders out, but he was approaching from inside, where it was a straight line to the third gate, behind which was the entrance to the secret passage. He shot one Syrian soldier, then another, inside the complex, and made a beeline for the third gate. That's when he heard a voice behind him.

"Stop right there, Boab!"

Robert froze. He recognized Lyosha's voice. The sound of small arms fire outside was becoming more intense.

"Drop your weapons!"

Robert let go of the Glock and slid the AK off his shoulder, letting it drop to the ground. He looked in Lyosha's direction, but all he saw was the blinding beam from his flashlight and the outline of four shadows.

"Kick them out of way."

He kicked the guns, one at a time, toward Lyosha.

"How did you know it was me? And that I'd be here?"

Robert knew Lyosha could drop him at any second. He was buying time, the only real commodity a man has.

"Nobody is good as you. I knew it was you when the general was hit."

"Are you going to shoot me?"

With his eyes on Robert, Lyosha picked up and pocketed the Glock, and then lifted and shouldered the AK. He stepped back shone the light down on the floor. Robert could see he was standing with three Syrian soldiers, who were all eager to shoot him.

"The general is already dead. I can't protect him anymore."

Lyosha looked into Robert's eyes. It was the look of a man who had failed. Robert's punishment should be death, but, at this point, it would also be a waste of an asset.

"You need me."

He clipped Robert's hands together with plastic ties, and then motioned to Robert with his rifle, and Robert trudged ahead. The popping of small fire became more intense and it was downright deafening by the time they had reached the end of the entrance complex.

A firefight was blazing in the old Ottoman streets outside. There was no defined front, with rebel guerillas simply attempting to wipe out whomever they saw, and Robert was no exception. Lyosha, Robert and the three soldiers crouched low, behind the foundation of an ancient villa.

"These are your people, Boab."

"They're not my people. My only target was the general."

"Right."

Lyosha knew that Robert was just a pawn they had used to get access to the citadel. He also knew Robert had no value as a prisoner. Not only would they not acknowledge him or his mission, now that they had their access, they could not care less if he lived or died. But he had killed the general and would have to answer for that crime.

They advanced toward the melee until they reached a clump of Syrian soldiers. Lyosha got into combat position, firing his rifle and commanding the Syrian soldiers. The rebels were firing on them, Robert included.

"Give me a gun."

"What?"

"Let me help."

Robert knew that Lyosha needed him and wouldn't turn down an extra gun.

"You are prisoner. Stay down and be quiet." Lyosha continued to fire until, all of a sudden, it became eerily silent, only a few pops of small arms in the distance. Suddenly, an RPG exploded the wall they were hiding behind and dozens of rebels rushed at them from the excavations. The soldiers shot some, but there were too many, and they kept coming. Before they knew it, they were in close quarters combat. Lyosha shot two with his sidearm, pulled out his combat knife and quickly approached Robert with it. Robert held out his hands and, with one sweep of his knife, Lyosha cut the ties. Lyosha then ducked behind a ruined wall. Robert turned over a dead Syrian soldier and took his knife and rifle.

While Lyosha was reloading, two rebels came at them, screaming. Robert shot them both before they had a chance to strike. Lyosha nodded to him. They were now in this fight together, and finally on the same side.

CHAPTER THIRTY-EIGHT

The rebels most likely had control of the visitors' center and who knows how many more had come in. Lyosha decided to double back and take up a position in the forward defensive tower, atop the throne hall that also happened to be an entrance to the second secret passage as well. They gathered up all the firing power of the downed soldiers, retreated to the entrance complex, and mounted the stairs to the tower. From there, they set up a perimeter and began to pick off pockets of their resistance. Lyosha radioed the other members of his *Spetsnaz* team.

He spoke to them in Russian, getting information on their positions and strength. Robert listened, curiously, unable to understand any of it.

"So what's happening?"

"It is report from Ramzes. Visitors' center is occupied by terrorists. We have one guy with sixteen soldiers in mosque of Abraham and another guy with eleven soldiers in Hammam Palace. And the soldiers on ring wall are still in place with their machine guns pointed in at the castle now instead of out."

"Where are your other two Russians?"

"Don't know. Probably dead."

"What is your plan?"

"In Spetsnaz, we all work together on plan. We are used to fighting behind enemy lines. I have told each team member to come up with strategy, then we all coordinate. Ramzes' idea is to parachute more forces into castle. That is how we usually get behind enemy lines."

"That's no good."

"Why not?"

"Because the rebels will shoot your guys before they hit the ground."

"We still have ring wall defenses that can cover them."

"Too risky."

"I think you are right. Other idea was to drop them in city, by entrance to tunnel."

"Not good enough. I have an idea."

"You are not member of team, but I listen."

"There are two structures higher than this one on the grounds. One is the mill and the other is the minaret of the big mosque. We've already seen muzzle flash from the mosque, so that's probably out, but I can go around the perimeter to the mill and take up a sniper position on the top of it. Then your guys from the Hammam and the mosque of Abraham can box the terrorists in the visitors center.

"I'll keep them away from the mill so we can seal off the secret passage and keep more of them from coming in and you call for air support to take care of the entrance to the tunnel on the street. Then you can drop your forces in to secure it. We can launch some of my fentanyl gas into the visitors' center and that should put most of them down. The rest we pick off on the outside from our tower and ring wall positions."

"Why would I trust you?"

"Because I'm the best sniper you have. You've already seen they're out to kill me, too. Besides, my escape path is right under us, not over on the other side. It would be suicide to try to escape through there with all the rebels coming in."

Lyosha nodded. "Go ahead. I set up plan. Just let me know when you are in place."

"I'm probably going to need some support."

"Take radio."

Lyosha unsnapped a radio unit from his belt and handed it to him.

"Air support?"

"No. They won't fire on citadel. It is international heritage monument. That would be war crime."

"That rules out artillery support as well."

"Right. We think of something."

"Okay, then."

They exchanged a mutual nod, and Robert left the tower, scurried down to the surface and became a part of the shadows. In the umbra he stayed close to the ring wall as he passed by the old arsenal, which was not too far from the Hammam, where Lyosha's other guys were holed up.

He continued along the ring wall, meeting no resistance, taking cover in the excavated areas, until he reached a virtual desert. Here, there had been no excavating, and the terrain was flat and exposed. Robert had only the darkness of the night and the thinness of the moon to count on. Other than that, he was a sitting duck.

CHAPTER THIRTY-NINE

Robert hugged close to the dusty stone wall, scanning the area ahead and on the side of him with his night vision goggles. As he readied himself to venture into the void, unprotected space, he thought of the grand battles that the soldiers who had lived, fought and died in and around the citadel had been a part of. In the distance, across the blackness he was about to cross, he could see, through his night vision goggles, the figures of men running about. They were not squads of organized soldiers.

They have to be rebels.

He was outnumbered and out-powered, yet, as he approached them, he felt invincible. He had been around the rebels enough to learn of the sophistication of their equipment. They were not equipped with night vision. He had the advantage. A calm resolve fell over him. His course was clear. He had no fear – that had long since left him. He continued his advance under cover of darkness and the dark contours of the castle's embattlements. He was one with the stone, the earth.

As he came closer to the mill, the chances of him being spotted increased exponentially. The entire group was moving toward the modern theater in the middle of the grounds, presumably on their way to the entrance complex, where the fight was. Robert kept on his course, steadily but carefully following the perimeter of the wall and keeping his night eyes on the rebels. Then, suddenly, a squad of five broke rank from the group and started running in his direction.

They've spotted me!

Robert hit the ground immediately, taking cover behind a large stone, and stayed calm and observed the situation. The squad stopped about 600 meters away, and fired on him. He could see the flashing explosions from their AK47s but, as he suspected, the bullets hit about 50 meters left of his position. He decided not to return fire – yet. They were still a little far from effective striking distance. All it would accomplish would be to alert them to his exact presence and then he would have several squads of rebels charging on him all at once.

It was just a rat, guys. A really big rat.

They stopped firing, and a long minute drew out as they held their positions.

Go back, guys, go back.

They didn't go back. Instead, they advanced toward Robert.

Now they're not sure if it was a rat or not.

Robert could either fight or run. He couldn't surrender – they would just shoot him. If he ran, he'd be on the defense and he would, most likely, be shot. If he fought, he could be shot as well, but he figured the odds were better if he stood his ground. The closer they got, the more effective his fighting would be. They kept coming, slowly and methodically although, like blind mice, they were headed in the direction of their fire, which would put them off course to his left if they went all the way to the ring wall. But, then they spread out to cover grids.

When they were about 400 meters out, he had two approaching him at twelve o'clock, one at one and two at nine. He radioed to Lyosha.

"Lyosha, I'm about 500 meters from the mill and a squad is approaching. I need a diversion."

"We see them, but we don't see you. Machine gunner will draw their fire."

Just then, two flares erupted above him, covering the entire area in a blanket of white light. At the same time, the gunner fired at the rebels with fury from the ring wall, they all fired back, instinctively, and Robert struck, shooting a deadly spray of bullets at the two at twelve and the one at one, cutting them down. The two at three o'clock hit the ground and started firing at Robert on automatic. He could hear the bullets hitting the ground all around him, pinging against the rock. It was impossible to look up to get a shot in, but he knew they weren't advancing, so he waited for them to change magazines.

Even if they were expert marksmen, it would take them at least three seconds to grab a new mag, release the spent one and slap the new one in. Robert waited for the telltale lull in the firing. The ring wall gunner was still firing on them, but they ignored him, and their compatriots were running to their aid.

The firing stopped, Robert rose up, took aim and fired, hitting the one on his left. The one on the right had reloaded and was firing back. Robert felt the impact on his body armor, which knocked him off, so his first shots didn't reach their purchase. He kept firing until the man went down, and the hot sting of another bullet grazed his shoulder.

The rest of the rebel platoon was headed his way, coming in hot. The gunner kept firing from the ring wall, but that wasn't going to help. Determined to stand his ground, he radioed Lyosha again.

"Need more support."

"Don't worry, helicopter coming."

"I thought you said they wouldn't fire on the citadel."

"No rockets, only machine gun."

The rebels kept coming, firing as they advanced. Robert waited until they were well within range and fired on them. He fired and fired, changed magazines and fired and fired again, and changed out mags again and kept firing.

Where's that fucking chopper?

They were dropping with Robert's fire, which slowed them down, but they kept coming, and he kept firing. Finally, down from the sky rained a destructive hell of heavy machine gun fire. He ran along the perimeter as he watched the copter fly away. But his path was still not clear. Advancing from the old barracks was another two squads of rebels.

CHAPTER FORTY

Robert put the radio to his cheek. "A little help here?"

"We see them, but we can't send helicopter – too close to archaeological site."

"What can you do?"

"We have gunner right above you. As soon as you are past him, he will fire on them."

Robert slinked past the gunner's position. He hit a pothole in the ground and tripped, but recovered his balance and kept running. When he was about 50 meters past him, the gunner started firing and the squad returned his fire. Flares exploded above his head in trails of smoke, raining down light, exposing Robert, and he began taking their fire. He fired back running as the bottom of the mill tower came into view. He ran and fired, changed mags while running and kept firing and firing. He could hear bullets whizzing all around him and saw fire flashing from the muzzles of their guns. He hit the ground behind a three-foot tall cornerstone. The chopper came roaring back overhead and shone its searchlight on the two squads. Robert aimed and fired, downing two of them in a fusillade.

He crawled the rest of the way to the base of the mill, feeling the grit in his eyes and nose and spitting dust out of his mouth. When he reached the edge of the base of the mill, a large group started at him from the visitors' center, firing as they ran. Robert fired back, reached the door and shot off the lock, knocked it in with his shoulder and climbed the stairs to the top. Anticipating unwanted guests, he slapped on his mask and exploded a gas canister in the stairwell.

As he reached the top, he flipped off the mask as a blast of fresh air and millions of stars greeted him. He tossed another gas canister down the stairwell, took a position on the south side, and began to pick off intruders, one by one, with precision. A rebel who was foolishly brave enough ran to the entrance of the mill and Robert shot him down. He sprayed the entire area with automatic fire and the rebels took to the ground in defensive positions.

He counted his clips – six. That meant he had 180 rounds left. He had to make every one count. Two bullets for every body – ninety bodies in all. He pushed the button on his radio.

"I've got the tower."

"We're coming."

Robert finally had a chance to catch his breath. He was soaked with sweat. As the warm breeze blew atop the tower, it cooled his skin. His arms ached and his trigger finger was bruised, even through the callouses. He looked out across the bailey. The troops had all dug in. A blanket of quiet fell over the citadel. The lull before the next battle.

CHAPTER FORTY-ONE

A rebel platoon was fast approaching the entrance complex, but was out of range of Lyosha's men and the ring wall gunners, and it was out of the question to send air support. Some of the most precious and completely restored structures were there and they couldn't risk their destruction.

During the lull, Lyosha's two spetsnaz team members advanced their squads: Ramzes from the Mosque of Abraham and Timon from the hammam. Robert could see them but they weren't in range for him to provide them any support. They would have to make it across the bailey on their own. Ramzes' group flanked left, confronting the advancing rebel group straight on, taking cover in the ancient streets and excavated dwellings. A machine gunner on the ring wall fired for Timon's group's cover as the sixteen kept advancing, drawing the attention of the sniper in the minaret, who fired on the gunner and he went down. Another gunner took his place and resumed firing.

Timon's group on the right engaged the advancing rebels as they moved forward from one excavation to another. Robert could see their advance but was in no position to help them yet. He was under attack himself, and heard bullets from potshots being taken at him whizzing by and pinging and pocking the stone mill around his position. He saw the culprit hiding behind a rock and kept an eye on him, his group advancing from the visitors' center and the doorway below. The rebel popped his head from the side of the rock. Robert quickly aimed and fired, but the head receded. He patiently waited for it to pop out again and, when it did, he aimed and fired again, and this time hit his aggressor. As he went down, Timon's group advanced, pushing back the rebels toward the visitors' center.

On the west side the battle continued at a standstill, with the guerillas taking shots at the small squad under cover of sniper fire. Five men, two with fentanyl canisters ran toward the mosque while Ramzes and another soldier covered them. Ramzes and the soldier took up positions and began firing, reloading and firing at the sniper's nest on top of the minaret, drawing return fire from the sniper.

"Go! Go!"

The five men double-timed it along the ancient streets as Ramzes and his man kept firing. When the sniper discovered all the firing was a decoy, it was too late – they had already reached the mosque, where they were in a firefight with its occupiers. They shot first one, then the second canister into the mosque. One rebel came running out, and they shot him down immediately. The sound of firing died down within the mosque, but the sniper was still up there. Two men began firing on the sniper while the three others ran inside to secure the mosque.

The mosque was secure. Ramzes exploded smoke canisters in the minaret stairwell and charged the sniper, killing him. He took over the sniper's position, covering the advance of Timon's men, who aggressively pushed on, forcing the rebels out into the open space between the visitors' center and the modern theater, and finally causing them to retreat into the center. There were still rebels firing upon them from the security of the old barracks, right under Robert's nose.

Timon and his men crossed the southern end of the modern theater with no casualties. They set up a center of operations behind the restrooms and prepared for a coordinated attack on the visitors' center and the old barracks. Lyosha radioed Robert.

"Ramzes is on top of minaret covering his squad. They will take visitors' center and Timon will take old barracks. We must cover them, on my mark."

Robert acknowledged Lyosha's call and stood prepared.

"Ready."

"On three! One, two, three!"

Robert and Ramzes showered the area with a barrage of fire upon both sides of the visitors' center, as Timon's group charged the old barracks, guns blazing. Robert began taking heavy fire from the windows of the visitors' center and, when the door on the east side opened, he realized why. Every time the rebels tried to exit the center to try to form a perimeter around it, Robert picked them off with a spray of automatic fire. Ramzes' men launched gas canisters into a window on the west side, and they stormed the center. Robert picked off three more rebels who attempted to escape from the east.

"Ramzes reports visitors' center secured. Calling for air strike on tunnel entrance."

Seconds later, Robert saw the chopper bearing down on the street below, laying down a fiery path of rockets. Timon's men, having secured the old barracks, threw a gas canister down the stairwell of the secret passage and charged into it.

"Passage secure! We have citadel!"

Robert didn't answer.

"Boab, come in. Boab?"

Robert had left the mill and was making his way back along the ring wall toward the entrance complex.

"Boab!"

Lyosha called Timon, asking him to dispatch two men to the top of the mill and waited their return call. When they got there, they confirmed what Lyosha had suspected. Robert had disappeared. Men like them think alike – mission first, survival always. He slammed the radio down in frustration.

CHAPTER FORTY-TWO

Robert anchored his line and threw it over the edge of the ring wall, where it disappeared into the darkness below. He rappelled himself down the wall, hit the slope, and then scurried to the south advance tower. Inside was another secret passage leading to the city, and the only means of escape he had left.

He slid down to the east wall of the advance tower, to prevent being seen by Lyosha and his men, and entered it. Robert shone his flashlight around, looking for the entrance to the secret passage.

It has to be here somewhere. Unless it's just a legend. God, I hope it's not a legend.

"It's here, Boab."

The voice in the blackness echoed and bounced against the empty stone. Robert switched off his torch, crouched down and followed its direction.

"Tower is also connected to entrance complex. I knew you would come here."

"Why don't you just look the other way?"

"You know I can't do that, Boab."

Robert kept softly shuffling toward the sound of the voice, but he still couldn't see anything, but Lyosha kept talking.

He always had a big mouth.

"I will shoot you, Boab. It is only way for men like us."

Robert felt the ground around him, picked up a stone and tossed it far to his right. Lyosha's flashlight lit up in the direction of its sound and Robert zoomed in on his coordinates.

"Very good, Boab. Old trick, but good."

The voice was moving. Robert tuned his ears in for sounds of physical movement. He followed every minute shuffle, until he could hear nothing but the silence of the dead air between them.

The silence was broken by the toss of another rock. This time Lyosha didn't buy it, but Robert heard the turn of his neck and the ruffling of his body armor. He was within striking distance so Robert struck straight at the sound.

It was a gamble, but it paid off. Robert slammed into Lyosha's body, knocking him down on his back. He heard the popping of gunfire as Lyosha's weapon discharged, sending random bullets echoing through the tower.

Both of them were down on the ground. Robert grabbed Lyosha's sidearm and twisted it against his trigger finger. He heard the snap of the finger breaking as Lyosha groaned in pain. Lyosha hit back with a left chop to Robert's wrist, dislodging the gun from his hand and it flew away. Robert stood up and Lyosha swept a leg across Robert's ankles and brought him down again, hard on the stone. Then, his legs came sliding across Robert's head like a snake slithering across it to wrap around his neck. Robert struck with his fist, nailing Lyosha's testicles. Lyosha cried out and released his grip. Robert scrambled to stand, sucking in dust and drips of sweat. It was like a battle of two Titan gods and it was not over.

Lyosha swung with a right, damaged fist, and Robert dodged the blow, swung back and caught Lyosha in the jaw. Lyosha hit back, aiming for Robert's throat, but catching his chin instead, sending him backwards. Robert shook off the pain and charged him with his head, nailing Lyosha in the abdomen, sending him down again. Robert jumped on top of him, and forced his knee against his chest, knocking the wind out of him. Lyosha grabbed his knife and Robert forced the knife hand to the ground with his left, putting pressure on his wrist until the knife was released, and swept it out of the way. He battered him in the face as Lyosha tried to recover with flailing arms, hitting Robert's sides.

Robert hit again and again and again, left, right, left, right, until it seemed like all the strength had gone out of Lyosha, like a tire losing all its air. He raised his arm, clenched his fist and aimed straight for Lyosha's nose, ready to deliver the kill shot. Lyosha suddenly opened his eyes and looked at Robert. It was a look of betrayal. A look that said they had fought together for survival, had become brothers, and now Robert had to uphold the code. Like a Samurai upholding the bushido, the code of a true warrior, Robert sensed in his eyes a relief that his death would come at the hands of a true warrior.

Robert, who was never one to show mercy to anyone, suppressed his killer instincts and, like an emperor in the Roman Coliseum, granted Lyosha a pardon. Satisfied that Lyosha was no longer a threat, Robert stood up, grabbed a flashlight from Lyosha's belt and his knife, and ran to the entrance of the tunnel. He screwed the noise suppressor onto his Glock and slumped forward. As he walked away he could hear Lyosha moan, "Nooooo!"

CHAPTER FORTY-THREE

Robert staggered down the stone stairs into the abyss, not knowing what the next surprise conformation may be. He was bruised and sore, bleeding from his superficial gunshot wound, and weary from the battle and the fight with Lyosha. The tunnel was cool and musty, and smelled like an ancient tomb, like the kind he had visited in the Valley of the Kings in Egypt. It felt like it hadn't been used in years.

It was smooth going for about 700 meters until he came upon an obstruction. He shone his light on it. The passage was completely blocked. It wasn't made by a cave-in by happenstance or an explosion. It was as if the rocks had been stacked together, like bricks in a brick wall, in order to block the passage. If it had been a collapse, it would have looked more random. This looked like a stone wall separating the fairways on a Scottish golf course. He quickly began removing the stones, throwing them behind him until he could feel the rush of air on the other side. He worked faster, picking stones with both hands and throwing them behind him. The hole was getting bigger and bigger. But, suddenly, he heard the sound of footsteps behind him.

Lyosha!

Robert had, so far, made a hole big enough for his shoulders. He tried to crawl through the hole like a cat, but got hung up on his body armor. The footsteps were getting closer. He threw his Glock and two mags through the hole, ripped off his jacket, his shirt, and the armor, and squeezed into it, scraping his arms and wiggling until he was stuck by the hips, wedged against jagged pieces of rock sitting on top of one another.

"Boab! Stoap!"

Robert planted his palms against the stone wall on the other side and pushed with all his strength, tearing his pants and ripping a layer of skin off his leg, just as he heard gunfire and the ricochet of bullets off the wall. He grabbed his gun and the mags and ran. There was no way Lyosha could get his bulky frame through the hole Robert had made. He would have to make a bigger one.

Robert ran as fast as he could from the breach in the wall. He could hear gunfire coming from it, and bullets ricocheting against the walls of the tunnel, but was well out of range without suffering a hit. He reached the tunnel exit, and creeped up the stone stairs into an abandoned building, and instinctively reached for his spy mirror, but his plate carrier and belt were gone. He twisted the silencer onto the muzzle of his Glock, peeked above the opening and saw a solitary guard. He shot, and he dropped to the dirt floor like a sack of potatoes.

Anticipating more guards outside, laying low to the ground, he peered out into the street on both sides. There was one solitary guard, standing watch, holding an AK-104. He snuck up behind the soldier, knife in his right hand, seized him by the neck, forcing it sideways, pierced the point of the knife into his throat and cut sideways, feeling the knife cut through tendons and flesh, and the warm flow of blood on his arm. The man fell, gurgling, blood spurting from his carotid artery. Robert picked up his gun and looked into the street. It was a no-man's land, but probably loaded with snipers. He turned to his left and ran to a destroyed wall, keeping close to it, then ran to the next one and the next one. There was nothing he could steal to make his escape. He would have to find where he had stashed the cycle.

CHAPTER FORTY-FOUR

The sun began to peek above the horizon, bathing the ruins of Aleppo in a yellow-orange glow. Robert hurried along the streets, mindful they could be filled with trigger happy rebels or Syrian patrols, both of which would shoot him on sight. He was tired and sore, bleeding from the leg and shoulder wounds and his mouth was dry, like it had been wiped out with cotton, crying out to quench his thirst. Bare-chested with torn pants, he looked like the Incredible Hulk after turning back into David Banner.

It was difficult to get his bearings, tough to look for landmarks in a city where every street seemed to be destroyed, but his fine-tuned stalking abilities were on full alert. He had calculated his location. If he went east, he risked running into bands of rebels. If he went west, he would run into Syrian patrols, which were probably on high alert, and possibly looking for him. He decided to take his chances going west. Syrian forces would be in uniform, more organized and traveling in groups. They would be easier to hide from than the rebels. The bike was northeast of the citadel, but it was in disputed territory. If there was one to steal, he would have opted for it.

He hung close to the destroyed buildings, keeping away from open spaces, scurrying through the ruins as he did in the citadel, from one burned-out, bombed-out wall to another. He could see the citadel looming above. It was aflutter with activity – helicopters flying overhead, illuminating the castle and its embattlements. He could hear the sounds of high-flying jets in the sky.

He entered the grounds of a large building, and came up on a street filled with a couple of burned-out cars and a disabled tank. He scanned the tops of the buildings for signs of snipers and scurried across the street. He took a convoluted route to avoid being anywhere near the citadel, turning what would have been a 17-minute walk into a 30-minute one.

The air was still and filled with the stench of garbage and the smoky smell of burnt wood. He kept on his meandering path, staying close to the buildings and using his roving eyes to keep aware of all his surroundings, walking at a normal pace.

At the next street crossing, Robert ducked down as a ragtag patrol of Toyota trucks came rolling by, which meant he was entering a patch of rebel territory. He lay low as they slowed and shone a spotlight in his direction. He could see the shadows shifting around him from the light. He stayed still, like he would if being charged by a dog.

Come on guys, there's nothing here for you.

***

It was midnight in New York, but Ted Barnard had still not gone to bed. He had been receiving intelligence reports all night about the citadel siege and his phone had never stopped ringing. It rang again and he put it to his ear. It was still hot from the previous calls.

"Barnard."

"Sir, this is Officer Jeffries."

"What have you got, Jeffries?"

"Reports from Aleppo that the rebels attempted a siege on the citadel but it was thwarted by the Syrian Army."

Barnard clenched his teeth. Any news on our asset?"

"Negative, sir. Assumed dead."

Barnard harrumphed. He could care less whether Robert had been killed, except for the dead American body which would have to be denied away. And, if Paladine wasn't dead, he should be.

***

Robert recognized the street and knew he was close to the hiding place for his motorcycle.

If it's even still there.

Robert entered the bomb-blasted area where he had covered his cycle with debris and, to his relief, it was still there. He excavated it from the rubbish and wheeled it slowly out to the street, where he kicked it to life and it whisked him away.

CHAPTER FORTY-FIVE

Nobody was waiting or standing by to pick Robert up, which was no surprise. This time there was no botched extraction because they obviously didn't expect him to make it, or they just didn't want him to. The whole mission stunk and, if he had his free will, he would have never been a part of it. He made up his mind right then and there he would take advantage of his presumed death and simply disappear. He cursed the man with no name as he made his way to the hole in the ground he used for storage. Once he got there, he grabbed a bottle of water and practically sucked it dry, then used the water from another bottle to splash his bloody and dirt-soaked face, arms and chest, and poured it on the surface wounds on his shoulder, arms and legs. There was no way he could present himself at the border crossing looking like a refugee or a battle-weary soldier. Cracking open his first aid kit, he took a large bottle of liquid antiseptic and dowsed his cuts with it. He changed into civilian clothes and packed everything back into his pack and saddled up again.

While the Commander of the U.S. Central Command was on television, denying U.S. involvement in the Aleppo siege, Robert was flying over moguls in the Syrian Desert, staying off the road as much as possible to avoid rebel and Syrian Army checkpoints.

He reached the border crossing of Bab al-Hawa in about an hour, scooting between the busy lanes, making a beeline for the border. As he approached the border crossing station, he looked at the overhang and its painted sign that said "Goodbye" and swore to never come back to this place.

Good riddance is more like it.

Crossing a border was always a nail-biting event for Robert, sometimes even more than an assignment, because, when you're entering another country, they control all the variables. You are a naked, worthless commodity which they decide whether they want or not, and the decision is usually made by a policeman who was put in the position of border guard because he wasn't good enough for anything else. This tended to give people a false sense of power. The good part about this border crossing, if there was one, was if there was any problem, the right amount of bribe could make that problem go away.

Robert presented his alias passport, the one with the Turkish visa already stamped in it, to the border policeman, a Turk, and greeted him in Turkish with a smile.

"Merhaba."

The man nodded, examined Robert's passport and visa and gave him a good look. Then, he stamped the passport and handed it back to him.

Robert headed straight for Iskenderun to wipe out his safety deposit box. He stopped on the way in a gas station restroom to clean up and make himself presentable for banking. Wary of any followers, he took special precautions, including "thanking" the bank manager for his business. The manager was a 30-something, ambitious Turk named Basri Demir, whose taste in clothes led Robert to believe he had taken special tips before. He greeted Robert and directed him to his private office. Robert declined.

"I think it's better we meet in the vault, if you don't mind."

Demir looked confused, then agreed. "Of course."

"You can understand my desire for complete privacy, can't you? The vault is a place where I feel that is possible."

"Yes, yes. That's fine."

Robert signed into his box for the last time and the manager took both keys to the vault while Robert watched from the door. Robert waited in the private room, where he had already disarmed the camera with his laser light. The manager brought the box in and set it on the table.

"Would you excuse me for a second?"

"Of course."

Robert emptied the contents of his box into his backpack and withdrew a brick of hundred dollar bills. He extended his hand to shake Demir's and when Demir met his gesture, Robert released the brick into his hand. Demir looked at it as if he were surprised.

"I just want to thank you for your service and discretion. I hope our banking relationship will continue in the future with complete discretion."

"Yes, sir. Thank you very much."

Demir pocketed the cash.

Robert held up a finger. "Oh, there's just one more thing."

"Yes, sir?"

"I need to be assured of the highest form of privacy. I wouldn't want anyone to be able to obtain my private records."

"Yes, sir, of course."

"Can you assure me you will take care of my privacy issue?"

"Yes, sir. I will handle it personally. No need to worry."

"Thank you."

"Can we offer you our car, sir?"

Robert shook his head. "Thank you for your hospitality."

Robert exited the bank and mounted his motorcycle for the eleven-hour ride to Istanbul.

CHAPTER FORTY-SIX

It was almost daybreak when Robert cruised into Istanbul. He took a hotel in the old town for cash – no name on the register. His footprints in Turkey had to be invisible – like tracks on the sandy beach, washed away by the waves. Robert showered, cleansing the rest of the battle grime and dirt from his body. After toweling off, he fell onto the bed and was asleep immediately.

He woke up two hours later, feeling partially rested, and headed straight for the Galata Bridge. The seagulls were calling, as if announcing his arrival. He passed the smoky, steamy fish grills of the *balik-ekmek* boats, where the waiters called out their famous fish sandwiches, until the smell of salt water and raw fish caught his nostrils. The fishermen were there, as always, sleeping on the benches and hanging over the rails with their fishing poles. Robert approached the grey-haired old man with the hat over his face.

"Dimitri!"

The old man slid off his hat, squinted and smiled.

"*Malaka*, you are back!"

Robert sat down next to him, and time seemed to take a vacation. They spoke for a while, but spent the rest of the time just hanging out. The old man took a hit of his nargile pipe, and offered the tube to Robert. Robert took in a sweet puff of ginger and mint, tasting it and blowing it out. Dimitri pulled in his line and rebaited his hook, then cast the line back out. He turned to Robert.

"You don't have a fishing pole or tackle box, *malaka*. That means you didn't come here to fish."

Robert nodded. "No, I didn't."

"And it looks like you have been in one hell of a big fight."

"Yes, I have."

"Then, how is it that this old Greek can help you, son?"

The old man was smart. Smart and wise.

"I need to get to Greece."

"It's close, no need to ask my advice."

"Not traveling there. I think I'm ready to retire. Greece is where I'd like to do it – in private."

The old man searched his eyes for the real question. He nodded and Robert could tell from the nod he understood.

"I see. With that, I'm sure this greasy Greek can help you. My nephew in my home town is in charge of resident visas."

"I think a passport would be better."

The old man ran scratched his moustache, thinking.

"Yes, that is also possible. Just a little more complicated. I assume this is a matter of utmost privacy?"

"Yes, it is."

"Then it will cost you, *malaka*. Not for me, but for the government man. Do you have ten thousand dollars cash?"

"I do."

"That should be sufficient. Bring it to me this afternoon, along with a standard passport photo. We should have your paperwork in a couple of days."

Robert nodded, but began worrying that, in a couple of days, a full scale manhunt could be launched for him. Dimitri sensed his angst.

"Don't worry about time, *malaka*. You can borrow a fishing pole and some tackle from me."

Robert smiled, put his pack on his lap, and pulled out his passport cover. Inside were several sheets of passport photos. He handed a sheet to Dimitri.

"You come prepared."

Robert reached back into his pack and pulled out five stacks of 100 bills, totaling $10,000.

"Don't you have to wave a magic wand over that bag first?"

The old man laughed roughly, and began to cough. He put his fist over his mouth. "Okay, *malaka*, here." He thrust the fishing pole into Robert's hands. "Anything you catch, we split fifty-fifty." Robert held the old man's pole and slid back on the bench.

***

The man with no name was finally back on U.S. soil, but he didn't feel secure. That Paladine was running around out there somewhere, he could feel it, and as long as he remained on the lam, he was a loose end. He didn't like loose ends.

He made some calls, but nobody in the field could confirm whether Robert was dead or alive. He had not popped up on any system alerts. He hadn't been seen anywhere. It was as if his trail had gone cold in Aleppo. He pulled up Robert's file on his computer and typed out an assignment to activate one of his best sleeper agents. Robert Garcia was out there somewhere and he had to be erased.

CHAPTER FORTY-SEVEN

Robert gripped the fishing pole and watched the old man throw a small fish over the side of the bridge. One of the seagulls, who had been circling in a mad, noisy flock of them, caught it in mid-air and the fishermen cheered. The old man sat back down on the bench.

"Today we pick up your passport and birth certificate."

"Already?"

The old man laughed in his hacking way. "I told you a few days was not a long time."

"I don't even know how long it's been. Seems like just yesterday."

"Then why don't you stay here, *malaka*?"

Robert scratched his head. "I'd like to, but."

The old man nodded. "Where will you go in Greece?"

Robert's eyes drifted off into the distance. "I'd like to just get on a boat and cruise the islands."

"Good idea. The islands are a place a man can disappear from life. It will be good for you, *malaka*."

Disappear. Not only good – necessary.

***

The staff at the NCTC were running around the high-tech center like molecules bouncing into one another, compiling data, making reports. Nathan Anderson's office was abuzz with activity, the boss scanning reports of alleged terrorists and barking out orders. With information came power, and his agency had compiled the largest database of potential terrorists in the world. Since he was the head of the agency, he felt that power, but also its responsibility. His pet project, the *Paladine Program*, was supposed to be the agency's poster boy. How to eliminate terrorism by striking out at the most notorious terrorists in the world. But he had become skeptical lately, wary of Ted Barnard at the CIA. He hadn't heard a word from Ted in days. And he hadn't heard much about PAL since his recovery after the Galeries Lafayette attacks. Out of frustration, he dialed Ted's number.

"Ted, Nathan Anderson."

"Oh, hello Nathan, how are you?"

"Everything's good, Ted, but I have to say I'm a little perturbed at not hearing from you."

"About what?"

"I expected to receive a report on PAL by now. Have you given him a new assignment?"

There was a pause on the phone. Barnard cleared his throat. "The PAL program has been suspended, Nathan."

"What? Why was it suspended? On whose authority?"

"It came from high up. All the way up."

"Why did nobody inform me?"

"Actually, you were my next phone call. You saved me the trouble."

Anderson's knuckles whitened as he clutched the phone, clenching his teeth. All the work, all the politicking, and now – nothing.

"Well, I think we should have a meeting about this to discuss it."

"Sorry, Nathan, but it's already done. The president likes his drone program. PAL is ancient history. The way of the past."

CHAPTER FORTY-EIGHT

The old man handed Robert a brown envelope. "Here are your documents, *malaka*. Everything official."

Robert took the envelope from Dimitri with his left hand and shook with his right. "Thank you, Dimitri."

"No need to thank me. This is what friends are for."

Robert bit his cheek. He was convinced he could never have a friend. He was not a good man. He knew he was one of the bad guys. Guys like Robert didn't have friends. All he had was the code. The code was king. His life meant nothing without it. But he appreciated the old man's help.

"I've got just one more favor to ask, but it may be kind of difficult."

"Ask, *malaka*. If it's too difficult, I will just refuse. My life is very simple, you know."

"I know."

***

Lyosha woke up in a dirty, dingy Syrian hospital. His head was pounding and the TV was blaring out some local program overhead. He called for help and a middle-aged Arab nurse walked in.

"Yes, sir?"

"I need to get out of here. Where are my clothes?"

She picked up his chart at the end of the bed and looked at it. "I'll have to call your doctor, sir."

"Forget about that. Just give me my clothes." He winced from the pain in his jaw when he spoke.

"You'll have to discuss it with your doctor."

"Could you at least turn off TV?"

"Yes, sir."

"And get me something for this headache."

"With a head trauma, it's important to evaluate your pain, sir. It helps us know what's going on."

Lyosha clenched his left fist and put it against his head. "What's going on is I have a fucking headache, now please get me those pills."

"Yes, sir."

She abruptly left and came back shortly after with some pills for Lyosha's headache. She put them on his tray with a glass of water and slid the tray closer to him.

"Your doctor is coming now, sir."

Lyosha took the pills and swallowed them. He gulped down the water like it was a shot of vodka. The glass felt funny in his lips, like after a trip to the dentist's office. A tall, lanky doctor with short-cropped hair, dressed in a white robe, entered the room.

"Hello, sir, I am Doctor Aboud. How can I help you?"

"Like I told nurse, I don't need help. I just want my clothes."

The doctor picked up the chart and flipped through it.

"You've been through a serious head trauma, sir. I'm afraid we have to ask you to stay with us a few more days for observation." He held a mirror to his face. "See?"

Lyosha looked in the mirror. His face had been battered, like a heavyweight boxer in a championship fight. It was bruised and bloody and there were bandages across the bridge of his nose. His lips were swollen, puffy and cracked. He swept away the mirror and gave the doctor a murderous glare. "I leave now. Get me my clothes, please."

The doctor gulped. "I'll tell the nurse to get your clothes for you right away, sir. But..."

"But what?"

"You'll have to sign a paper that you're leaving against my advice."

"Give me paper, I sign."

CHAPTER FORTY-NINE

Svetlana Ivanova's doorbell rang and she ran to open it. When she did, all she could see was white chrysanthemums and red roses – dozens and dozens of them. They seemed to fill the entire doorway. She heard a young man's voice behind them.

"Svetlana Ivanova?"

"Yes."

"Delivery for you."

"I see, please just give them to me."

The man handed her the huge bouquet.

"Thank you."

"There is more."

"What?"

He handed her a clipboard with a pen attached to it. "Please sign here."

She signed, he thanked her, and left. She closed the door, smiled and lifted the flowers to her face, breathing in their scent. She went to the kitchen to fix them and set them down on the counter. She opened the cabinet and pulled out the largest vase she could find, and opened the drawer and pulled out a pair of scissors. She looked through every stem, wondering if there was a card or something that would tell her who they were from. Lifting up the flowers, she saw a tiny card drop out onto the counter. She opened it. In Russian, was written: "Thinking of you, Bob."

She smiled and held the flowers to her breast and she thought of Bob, wondered where he was and what he was doing, and that she would probably never see him again.

CHAPTER FIFTY

The little boats bobbed up and down, like apples in a carnival game, dancing together and rocking as the waves lapped the small harbor of the tiny Greek Island of Spetsas. Robert fired up the engine of the *Lana,* a small 10-meter boat, secured the cabin door and checked the rig lines, pulling them out of their cleats and off the winches. He casted off the moor lines and eased the Lana out of its space.

He cruised out past the harbor speed limit and into the open sea, pointed the boat in the direction of the wind, killed the motor and hoisted the mainsail. As it flapped in the wind, he raised the jib, which filled with air. The wind caught both sails and sent the boat flying across the water, leaning with speed. He held his hand on the wheel as he looked out to sea. It was a sunny day, but cold, and the misty sea breeze stung against his face as he wrapped his jacket closed. He could taste the salt in the breeze and licked his lips.

Destination? Anywhere.

Robert sailed. He sailed and sailed until he felt like he was one with the wind, completely free. When the wind finally died, he looked over the side into the crystal clear water. The sun illuminated the first few meters and then it turned a deep blue. He opened his tackle box, and sat down in his deck chair, fixing the line and baiting his hook. He cast his line out and leaned back in the chair. Time had ceased to exist. When the wind finally picked back up, Robert awoke from a "fishing snooze" and looked down at his bucket. It was full of fish. He was finally home.

EPILOGUE

The old man slouched on the bench, dreaming peaceful dreams, mostly of beautiful girls. As he was kissing one, something cold, wet and slimy brushed against his chin, then he opened his eyes to a blinding light as the hat fell to the pier. A huge pink tongue was licking his face.

"What do you want, you ugly old dog?"

The dog sat down and hung his head, looking guilty.

"Are you hungry?"

He wagged his tail. The old man pulled a filet of angler fish from his icebox and threw in the air, and the dog caught it immediately and gulped it down like a seal.

"Bob was right about you. You're a real pain in the ass."

The dog just wagged its tail and panted, its long tongue dripping.

AFTERWORD

I began writing this novel during the most bizarre election campaign in history between two of the most unpopular candidates ever to win the nomination of a major political party in the United States. At first, I thought I could make a choice between the two; select the lesser of the two evils; but then the propaganda wheels for the military industrial complex started spinning stories about Russia preparing for nuclear war. It soon became clear to me that "We came, we saw, he died."[1] Hilary Clinton's Russia bashing was a prelude to the workup of a new cold war to justify billions in government contracts for arming Europe and possibly the Ukraine. This essay is not to be interpreted as slanted "liberal" or "conservative." I am just noting what I observed.

After World War II, the United States economy had to shift from a wartime to peacetime economy. However, that left the defense industry, which had been the driving force behind the wartime economy, out to dry. They needed an enemy. Thus, the "cold war" was begun with the Communists as the enemy.

Fast forward to the 21st Century. No more Soviet Union, no more Communist threat. Vacillating Donald Trump at first declared NATO obsolete, but then tried to tweet himself out of it.[2]

But Trump was not the first one to declare NATO obsolete. Putin himself declared in 2014 that NATO was part of the old "bloc" system and had outlived itself.[3] The real-life setting of this novel in civil war-torn Syria is a perfect example of how "Spy vs. Spy" can be a very dangerous game.

In 2016, the United States Treasury opened a terrorism finance inquiry into a large number of brand new Toyota trucks being used by ISIS. The U.S. State Department and the British government had both provided the "Free Syrian Army," a loose group of rebels who had expressed a desire to topple the al-Assad government, with the trucks, which were now being used by Islamic terrorists.[4]

In 2016, in the northern province of Aleppo, different groups fighting the Syrian civil war are vying for the same territory, among them the Free Syrian Army, the U.S.-armed Kurdish YPG, and ISIS. Free Syrian Army officials have cited a "deepening divide" between themselves and the Kurds, with the Kurds stating they could probably eliminate the FSA in a war. Many other groups fighting in the area include the Martyrs of Syria Brigade, the Northern Storm Brigade, an Islamist FSA unit, the Islamic Front, which welcomes jihadist fighters, and the Syrian Islamic Liberation Front.[5]

U.S. Special Forces Officer Jack Murphy reported in September 2016 that the U.S. policy of aiding Syrian rebels had the Special Forces training and arming Syrian anti-ISIS forces, while the CIA was maintaining a parallel program to arm anti-Assad insurgents. Murphy reported that distinguishing between former al-Qaeda affiliate al-Nusra and the Free Syrian Army (supported by the CIA) was impossible, and that, as early as 2013, FSA commanders were defecting to al-Nusra, while still retaining the FSA moniker to maintain access to CIA-provided weaponry. He also reported among the rebels that

U.S. Special Forces and Turkish Special Forces were training, at least 95% of them were either working in terrorist organizations or supporting them. This would lead credence to Russia's contentions that the Syrian rebels are no more than terrorists themselves.[6]

Witnesses describe Syrian rebels in Aleppo, including the FSA, al-Nusra, Ahrar al-Sham and Nour el din Zinki, as terrorists themselves.[7] In July 2015, Syrian rebels blew up the western gate of the UNESCO protected heritage site, the Citadel of Aleppo with underground explosives.[8] The U.S.-backed rebels, who are now fighting the Russians in Syria, have blown up the Carlton Hotel and the Palace of Justice in the same manner. Aleppo itself is almost completely destroyed.[9]

So, it seems not only is the choice of who to support a mess, as it usually has been with interventions in Afghanistan and Iraq, but the United States and Russia are fighting a proxy war against each other. There are so many factions fighting for their own individual objectives in the Syrian civil war it is difficult to sort them all out. What is sure, however, is that Russians were the only ones invited by the legitimate Syrian government.

I don't condone or support genocide or terrorism. However, I don't think regime change is the proper paradigm to follow. Call Vladimir Putin a dictator if you may, but his idea of stabilizing the war and then calling for free, monitored elections seems saner to me than arming and training different factions of rebel groups and then having to fight the same groups you have armed with American lives.

One more thing...

I hope you have enjoyed this book and I am thankful you have spent the time to get to this point, which means you must have received something from reading it. I would be honored if you would post your thoughts, and also leave a review. Please also feel free to share your thoughts about the book or any of my series by sending an email to: info@kennetheade.com. I love to hear from readers, whether it is bad or good.

Best regards,

Kenneth Eade

BONUS OFFER

Sign up to receive another one of my books free, paperback discounts, advance sale notifications of books and monthly giveaways by visiting my website: http://www.kennetheade.com/free-download/. I will never spam you.

AND THE ADVENTURE CONTINUES WITH BOOK 3

Sacrifice, charity, and concern for others has always been a characteristic of the human spirit. But there is a wild, hungry, thirsty, selfish creature that lurks deep within the libido of each of us. That *id* some of us ignore, others deny, and still others put a mask on it or lock it away so even they cannot release it. But when the balance is tipped to its side, it can break any bonds that have tied it down, and we are powerless to stop it. The result can be exhilarating, intoxicating, mind-blowing, or it can be deadly.

Robert Garcia had run away from himself, had tried to convince himself that his past was not a part of his present.

"Normal" people work thirty years at a "regular job" and then they retire on a small pension and Social Security. Robert never had a job that could be called normal. Like his father, he had sought a career in the military and the pinnacle of his career had been a position with the elite Special Forces of the Army – formerly known as the Green Berets. But it was covert operations where Robert's intensive training and exceptional warfare skills were put to their highest and best use. Robert was a terminator – a fine-tuned, killing machine, the product of intensive training and many years of death-dealing assignments. His last job was one that had nearly marked the end of his life – a dangerous life to Robert and to anyone around him. But now, there was nobody close to him. For Robert, that was the only way to survive.

He thought he had finally found a way to retire from the life of an assassin in one of the oldest activities known to man – fishing. He'd saved up a nice chunk of money from lucrative assassination jobs and had bought himself a little sailboat. He had never been a philosopher, nor had he ever been a sportsman, but there was something about floating on a little boat in the middle of a nameless sea, casting out a line and kicking back that suspended all time and reality. This anonymous life he had chosen of living on the water, cruising the obscure Greek islands, and creating a home for himself as a hermit on the tiny island of Spetses took him away from a reality that would be far too horrid for any normal person to endure. The trouble with Robert was that this idyllic life of Homer was not his, and it didn't take long for the beast that he had locked away to rattle its cage with frustration. It was tired of fishing and wanted to come out to play.

From his little sailboat in the port he could see the horse-shoe-shaped harbor of Porto Heli, a summer resort area packed with revelers and partiers, and more easily accessible to him than the party island of Mykonos. It was about a 30-minute cruise. His island was dark, quiet – like Robert was. The sidewalks rolled up at 10 p.m. Night life was practically non-existent. As he sat on the deck and looked out across the sea, he was drawn to the twinkling lights of Porto Heli like a fly to a porch light. The lapping of the water against the little boats as they bobbed up and down, the sound that used to soothe him to sleep so many nights in the cabin of the bow of his boat, the *Lana,* now grated on his nerves like fingernails dragging against a chalkboard. Finally, he couldn't take it anymore. He started the motor of the *Lana*, cast off the mooring lines, and, just like that fly, headed straight for the light.

It was a short ride that divided the two worlds; the one of the people by day and the other of the people by night. The day people worked, played, laughed and ate, and then they slept, resting to start the cycle all over again. The night people, on the other hand, lived only for thrills, and their object was to have as much fun and pleasure as they could before the sun rose.

As he neared the harbor, he could hear the sounds of partying in the bars and began to ache with impatience – like a dog salivating for a bone. He threw the fenders over the side, cut the motor and pulled alongside a concrete pier and a man came out, tossed him the mooring ropes and he quickly looped them over the cleats. He locked up the boat, hopped off and handed the man a fifty euro bill.

"I'll probably be a few hours."

The man slipped the bill into his pocket and smiled a checkerboard smile of half a mouthful of stained teeth. Robert had made his own price because it was late and the money would probably not be accounted for.

"No problem."

"Make sure nothing happens to my boat and there'll be another fifty in it for you."

The man smiled again and nodded.

Robert followed the sounds of the action like the pack of rats followed the Pied Piper of Hamelin. His will was no longer his own; he had given it up to the beast, and it was the beast who would be calling the shots tonight. It didn't take long to find the best party. He followed the pulsating beat of electronic music to Nikki Beach Resort. As he came nearer, he could see what was a seaside patio for sun bathers by day had turned into a dance floor at night, illuminated by sparkling fountains of fire, casting flickering shadows against the dancers, most of them female.

As Robert approached, he saw the bouncer, a big man with no neck, rustling a man out of the club. The guy he was handling was well dressed, but he was obviously drunk, so the bouncer had the right to evict him. But he didn't stop after he had "bounced" the man. He went a step further – a step too far. He pushed him out onto the sidewalk, and the man fell. The man struggled to get up, and, when he did, the bouncer kicked him down.

This wasn't Robert's battle, so he decided to play it cool. Unfortunately, however, the bouncer wasn't content to end the drama with one kick. Robert observed, quietly, while the bouncer continued to rough up the drunken man, pushing him around and slapping him down. Some people, of certain strength, take pleasure in pushing around others with none. The bouncer was probably a bully when he was a kid. Now, he was a grown-up bully, and one with authority.

"Hey, man, you kicked him out. Why don't you just let him go?"

The bouncer looked up at Robert as if he had thrown down a gauntlet. He had tasted blood and here was another fight.

"You want a piece of this?"

"No, man. I'm just saying this guy's had enough."

The big-necked man grabbed Robert by the collar and came nose to nose with him. Robert could feel his hot, bad breath against his face.

"You will take your hands off me and do it now."

"Or what, big man? You gonna beat me up?"

The beef-neck began to laugh, tightening his grip. Like a snake, Robert struck, pushing him back, then slamming him in the nose with a loud crack.

"Nobody touches me."

The man's hand instinctively went to his nose, and then he looked at his bloody palms with anger. He sized Robert up, hurt now only in his pride. By that time, another bouncer had joined him. They looked like two lion statues, the kind rich people put to mark the entrance of their driveways. The beast had been awakened in Robert, who stared them down with cold, shark-like eyes.

"Now let's try this again. I don't want any trouble. I'd like to have a drink, maybe meet some girls and try to get laid tonight. Or I can beat the living shit out of both of you. I'll get an equal amount of a different kind of satisfaction out of either activity. It's your move."

ABOUT THE AUTHOR

Described by critics as "one of our strongest thriller writers on the scene," author Kenneth Eade, best known for his legal and political thrillers, practiced International law, Intellectual Property law and E-Commerce law for 30 years before publishing his first novel, "An Involuntary Spy." Eade, an award-winning, best-selling Top 100 thriller author, has been described by his peers as "one of the up-and-coming legal thriller writers of this generation." He is the 2015 winner of Best Legal Thriller from Beverly Hills Book Awards and the 2016 winner of a bronze medal in the category of Fiction, Mystery and Murder from the Reader's Favorite International Book Awards. His latest novel, "Paladine," a quarter-finalist in Publisher's Weekly's

2016 BookLife Prize for Fiction and finalist in the 2017 RONE Awards. Eade has authored three fiction series: The "Brent Marks Legal Thriller Series", the "Involuntary Spy Espionage Series" and the "Paladine Anti-Terrorism Series." He has written eighteen novels which have been translated into French, Spanish, Italian and Portuguese.

OTHER BOOKS BY KENNETH EADE
Brent Marks Legal Thriller Series
A Patriot's Act

Predatory Kill

Trial by Terror

Arresting Resist

Killer.com

Assumed Innocent

To Remain Silent

Decree of Finality

Beyond All Recognition

The Big Spill

And Justice?

Involuntary Spy Espionage Series
An Involuntary Spy

To Russia for Love

Stand Alone
Terror on Wall Street

Paladine Political Thriller Series
Paladine

Russian Holiday

Traffick Stop

Unwanted

[1] Clinton's comments (on the air) upon hearing of Muamar Gaddafi's brutal torture and murder.

[2] Jacobson, Louis, Donald Trump mischaracterizes NATO change and his role in it, Politifact, August 16, 2016

[3] Weiss, Michael, when Donald Trump was more anti-NATO than Vladimir Putin, The Daily Beast, November 4, 2016

[4] Cartalucci, Tony, The Mystery of ISIS' Toyota Army Solved, New Eastern Outlook, 2016

[5] Mishgea, Syrian Madness: US Backed Rebels Fight US Special Forces, June 25, 2016, Mishtalk

[6] Crooke, Alistair, U.S. Special Forces Officer: How the CIA armed and trained jihadists for war in Syria, Consortium News, September 29, 2016

[7] Bartlett, Eva, The Villages in Aleppo Ravaged by America's "Moderate" Rebels, Global Research, September 29, 2016

[8] Sputnik, Militants detonated a tunnel under the western gate of the citadel, July 7, 2015, Sputnik International

[9] Lamb, Christina, The Australian, Rebels resisting Russian backed troops in Syria

Made in the USA
Las Vegas, NV
24 October 2020